I0653445

CAULDRONS
and
CATS

Familiar Spirits - Book 2

CHRISTINE POPE

This is a work of fiction. Names, characters, places, and incidents are either the product of the author's imagination or are used fictitiously. Any resemblance to actual events, places, organizations, or persons, whether living or dead, is entirely coincidental.

CAULDRONS AND CATS

Copyright © 2023 by Christine Pope

ISBN: 978-1-946435-65-1

Published by Dark Valentine Press

Cover design by Danielle Fine

Ebook formatting by Indie Author Services

All rights reserved. No part of this book may be reproduced in any form or by any electronic or mechanical means, including information storage and retrieval systems—except in the case of brief quotations embodied in critical articles or reviews—without permission in writing from its publisher, Dark Valentine Press.

Chapter 1

The Cat and the Conundrum

"Shelby is *not* my fiancée!" my not-quite-boyfriend Noah said, brows pulled together in a fierce scowl, probably the most forbidding expression I'd ever seen him wear. Usually, he looked friendly and open, with his bright blue eyes and thick brown hair that always seemed just a little bit tousled.

He stood a few paces away from the spot where I'd been yanking weeds in my herb garden, hands jammed in the pockets of his khakis. I wasn't sure exactly why I'd retreated to the backyard ten minutes ago when I'd gotten home after being confronted by Shelby Howard on Noah's doorstep, only that it had seemed a good idea for me to be venting my fury on the plants outside where I could at least get some fresh air.

"Oh, really?" I said, my frosty tone about forty

degrees colder than the mild late-May breezes that flowed through my expansive backyard on their way inland from the Atlantic. It was almost six o'clock, but the sun wouldn't set for a few more hours, and the warmth of the day still lingered. "Then do you mind telling me why Shelby introduced herself that way?"

Because it wasn't as though I'd hallucinated the whole episode. No, I'd gone over to Noah's house, trying to figure out why he'd canceled our dinner date when it had been several days since we'd last seen each other and he'd seemed eager for us to finally have a real evening out together. Unfortunately, Shelby Howard had been the one who'd opened the door in answer to my knock, and who'd informed me that she was his fiancée. I'd stared at her in shock for a second or two, then recovered myself enough to stammer something silly about needing a refill for my dog's medication before I beat a hasty retreat to my battered but trusty Land Rover Discovery where it waited at the curb.

I hadn't even been halfway home to my vintage house on Winter Island Drive before my cell phone started ringing, but I'd resolutely ignored it. No, I'd kept driving, pulled my car into the garage, and stalked into the house, fuming.

How could he have neglected to tell me about something like that?

Because Noah had never come right out and

told me he was unattached. No, he'd just played Mr. Nice, helping me when Milo, the cocker spaniel familiar I'd been watching, was dognapped, being generally supportive and acting like an all-around good guy. There was absolutely no way in the world I could have ever suspected he was hiding such a big secret.

And okay, a neutral observer might have pointed out that I was keeping just as big a secret from him, that I'd made sure he couldn't possibly know I was a witch whose shop in downtown Salem, Full Moon Apothecary, was a little bit more than simply a store where people could buy herbal remedies for insomnia and arthritis.

Our situations were entirely different, though. The entire witch community had to work very hard to make sure the rest of the world didn't know anything about our powers. I couldn't tell Noah the truth about me—or the rest of the witch world—until I was damn sure he was going to be a permanent fixture in my life.

Considering he had a fiancée he'd been hiding from me, I kind of doubted that was ever going to happen.

Noah ran a hand through his hair, mussing the thick, wavy locks. He was a little over six feet tall, broad-shouldered, and with piercing blue eyes the color of the purest summer sky. Right now, though, those gorgeous eyes were narrowed, and just the faintest flush touched his sculpted cheekbones.

"Because she's nuts," he said, then checked himself, as if he'd realized as soon as the words left his mouth that describing a former significant other in those kinds of unflattering terms probably wasn't a very good look. He released a breath, then went on, "Look, Charity, I figured I'd get around to telling you about Shelby at some point, but since she wasn't currently a part of my life, I thought I could wait a little longer."

I shoved my clippers into a pocket of the gardening apron I wore, then crossed my arms. A few yards away, Milo, the spaniel familiar I'd basically adopted after his former mistress was murdered, appeared to be asleep under an oak tree. However, even though he gave every appearance of a dog dead to the world, I had a feeling he was listening to every single word Noah and I were saying.

Whatever. It wasn't as though Milo and I had any secrets from one another. No, he wasn't my familiar in the strictest sense of the word—we probably would never share the kind of bond that most familiars had with their mistresses, simply because he hadn't chosen me at an early age—but he was also much more than simply a pet. I'd made the decision to have him become a part of my life, and that meant he needed to know everything that was going on in my world.

No matter how awkward it might be.

"Exactly how long *were* you going to wait?" I demanded, and Noah shoved his hands into the pockets of his creased khakis.

"I don't know," he said, his tone sharpening a bit. "Maybe until we'd gotten at least one or two real dates under our belts."

"Like the one you canceled last night?"

His brows drew together, but he looked more annoyed than angry. "I didn't have much choice," he replied, "considering the way Shelby showed up out of nowhere last night. I didn't know how long it was going to take to get rid of her, so I figured it was safer to postpone our date until she'd gone back home."

"Which is in Boston?" I inquired, my voice still tight. Noah had told me a few days earlier that he'd grown up in Boston and gone to school there, so I guessed that was where Shelby must be from as well.

"Yes," he said, then paused. He glanced over at the spot where Milo was sleeping under the oak tree, and added, "Do you mind if we go inside and talk about this?"

I wanted to retort that there wasn't anything more to say, but I knew that was a knee-jerk reaction and nothing more. No, I needed to recognize that, even though Noah's and my relationship had been in its very beginning stages, we definitely shared the kind of chemistry I'd never experienced with anyone else. Ignoring our connection just because I was hurt and angry didn't seem like a very good idea.

"All right," I said, knowing I sounded way too grudging. "Come on in."

Without waiting for him to respond, I turned away and started walking toward my home's back door, the one that opened into the kitchen. Noah's firm footsteps as I walked into the house told me he'd followed almost immediately behind me.

However, he paused on the back step and sent a quick look over one shoulder before saying, "Is it all right to leave Milo outside?"

Maybe Noah was thinking of how the dog had been attacked in that very same backyard by a monster who'd actually been a man born with witch powers, an unheard-of anomaly in my magical world. However, because that man—Brian Alatorre—was now dead, I didn't think Milo had anything to worry about.

"He'll be fine," I said. "When he wants in, he'll use the doggy door."

Noah nodded, then went ahead and closed the back door. Doing so wasn't strictly necessary, since I had a permanent spell in place on my home's rear entrance to ensure any marauding bugs stayed out in the yard where they belonged, but I couldn't exactly tell him that.

"Some iced tea?" I asked next, figuring I should at least attempt to be polite.

"Sure," Noah replied at once. The halfway relieved expression he wore told me he was glad my request had been so innocuous.

I went ahead and poured glasses of tea for us, then said, "Let's go into the living room."

He didn't protest, only followed me into the space, which looked way too cheerful for such a fraught conversation. A vase full of daisies and Queen Anne's lace cheered up the mantel, and the white-painted furniture and blue and yellow-upholstered couch and chairs made the room look bright and friendly on even the darkest winter days.

Maybe the décor didn't need as much of a boost on a warm May late afternoon like this one, but still, I found myself relaxing just the littlest bit as I settled myself on the couch.

Noah had obviously realized he probably shouldn't take any liberties with things so tense between us, so he sat down on one of the armchairs that faced me. "I know this looks terrible," he said, "but I'm telling you the truth. Shelby and I split up more than a year ago, and I haven't even talked to her since I moved here to Salem. Last I heard through a mutual friend, she'd already gotten engaged again. A guy named Trevor Miller."

This revelation made me raise an eyebrow. "If she's engaged to someone else," I returned, "why the hell was she answering your door and introducing herself as your fiancée?"

"She told me it was a mistake," Noah replied.

"A 'mistake'?" I repeated, thinking that sounded like a load of bull if I'd ever heard one.

He swallowed some of the iced tea I'd poured for him. A delaying tactic, or did he just have a bad case of dry mouth?

Either way, he didn't pause for very long. "She said something about just blurting it out, that being here with me must have gotten her thinking it was like old times again...or something like that." His mouth twisted, and he added before I could speak, "Yeah, I know it sounds ridiculous, and I told her that."

"So," I said, "if she's engaged to this Trevor guy, then what is she doing here in Salem?"

To his credit, Noah didn't hesitate. "That's the problem," he replied at once. "They broke up. She wouldn't say why. She only told me she'd made a horrible mistake in dumping me a year ago when I decided to leave Boston and move to a smaller town, and that she wanted to try to patch things up between us."

I couldn't help frowning. No, I wasn't exactly thrilled about Noah having an old flame turn up out of nowhere. Beyond that, though, I couldn't help having a pretty low opinion of a woman who sounded as if she couldn't bear to be alone for any appreciable length of time.

No wonder she'd introduced herself as Noah's fiancée, even if it was sounding more and more as though that reality existed in her mind and nowhere else.

"And you told her...?" I ventured, hoping I didn't sound too invested in his reply.

"I told her it was over between us, and she needed to go back to Boston and either patch things up with Trevor or start working on herself and try to figure out why she has such a pathological avoidance of being on her own."

Pretty much exactly the same thing I'd been thinking only a moment earlier, thus proving that I hadn't been fooling myself when I'd thought maybe...just maybe...Noah Jenkins might be the guy I'd believed I would never find.

He'd been facing me directly during that entire speech, jaw tight, gaze forthright. No, I didn't have any particular skill at being able to determine whether someone was telling the truth or not— well, not without casting a spell to do the heavy lifting for me—but sometimes you didn't need magic, only clear body language.

When I spoke again, my tone was much gentler than it had been a few minutes earlier. "And...now what?"

The tense set of his shoulders eased just a little. "Now...." He paused, and released a breath. "I told her if she didn't want to go back to Boston right away, if she needed some time to figure out things between her and Trevor, that was all right, but she couldn't stay with me any more than that first night, since she showed up too late to find a room." Another hesitation, a little more pronounced than the previous one, and he went on, "This morning before I left for work, I told her I was seeing someone and that it would be too strange to have her there at the house, even if she was just staying in my guest room. And I told her to start looking online for a hotel. I don't know if she found one, because that's when I left and came straight over here."

For a moment, I wasn't sure what to say. That Noah had told Shelby he was seeing someone meant a lot to me, especially because we still hadn't even had what you could call an official "date."

And I had to believe if he didn't care...if he didn't think some kind of a future was possible between us...then he wouldn't have come rushing over to my house to clear the air.

In short, even though I'd been burning with a fury to match my red hair only a few minutes earlier, I found myself cooling down pretty darn quickly.

"I'm sorry you had to deal with this," I said, and he gave a resigned shrug.

"Honestly, seeing her again just made me that much gladder we broke things off," he responded. "Still, she was a part of my life once, and I thought I should at least wait a little to see if she could find someplace to land."

"That's awfully nice of you," I said, wondering if I would have been that generous with any of my exes.

But I'd never been engaged to any of them, had never had a relationship that lasted longer than a couple of months. Being a witch was hard that way, since you had to be absolutely, positively sure that someone was your soul mate, the person you were going to spend the rest of your life with, before you could reveal to them that you were a witch and tell them anything about the magical world that had been carefully hidden from regular society for hundreds—if not thousands—of years.

I'd never met anyone I'd thought could be that person for me.

Well, not until Noah, anyway.

He drank some more iced tea. "She's in a bad place," he said. "She was kind of her dad's little girl, and he passed away from pancreatic cancer last year. I got the feeling she latched on to Trevor Miller because he was a little older, someone who made her feel safe."

Because I didn't have a father—well, except in the purely biological sense, since I'd been conceived via artificial insemination—I couldn't really relate. All the same, it sounded to me like Shelby needed some serious psychological counseling rather than using her former fiancé as a daddy surrogate.

However, I kept those thoughts to myself. I didn't know the woman, and I also didn't want to sound like the kind of person who needed to badmouth someone else in order to make herself look better.

"And that's why I thought it might be a good idea for her to hang out in Salem for a while, just to try to clear her head," Noah continued. "As long as it's not at my place," he added quickly, lest I got the wrong idea.

Considering it was Sunday evening of Memorial Day weekend, I didn't know how much luck Shelby would have on that front. True, people would probably be heading out tomorrow so they'd be home in time to be back at work on Tuesday morning, but that didn't help much with finding a place to stay tonight.

Except....

Hannah Owens, a witch in my coven—although she often skipped our ceremonies, claiming to be too busy—had a cottage around the corner from my friend Stella's tea shop that she rented out on both Airbnb and VRBO. It had been booked this weekend, but I'd heard through the witchy grapevine that her guests had canceled at the last minute due to family illness. Because the cancellation had come right before the holiday, there hadn't been time to find someone else to fill it.

Which meant the little cottage was probably the perfect place for Shelby to stay while she tried to get her life figured out. In fact, I had a feeling Hannah would give her a great deal just so the weekend wouldn't be a total loss.

"I think I know where Shelby can stay," I said, and then explained about the cottage. "Let me give my friend Hannah a call."

The visible relief on Noah's face would have been almost comical—if it weren't that we both had a vested interest in making sure Shelby was holed up someplace safely out of the way so she wouldn't interfere with...well, whatever was going on between the two of us. "That would be great," he said. "Thank you for doing this."

I couldn't help smiling. "Well, this is just as much for my benefit as it is for Shelby's."

He actually chuckled at that comment, telling me he'd already begun to relax a bit.

Since I had my phone in one of the other pockets of my gardening apron—I really should've taken it off when I came in the house, but had been way too preoccupied—it was easy enough to pull it out, go through my contacts list to find Hannah's entry, and then make a quick call. She was over-joyed to hear she'd have a guest tonight and for at least two or three nights after that.

"But I've got guests coming on June ninth," she warned me. "So if your friend is still in Salem by then, she'll need to find somewhere else to go."

Considering June ninth was almost two weeks away, I had to hope that Shelby would have her life figured out by that point, or at least would have headed back to Boston to have a sit-down with Trevor. I assured Hannah that I doubted Shelby would be staying in Salem for that long, and finished up by saying we'd have her over at the cottage sometime within the hour.

After I ended the call, I told Noah, "I hope that's okay. I don't want Shelby to feel like we're springing this on her."

"No, it's fine," he replied at once. "I mean, I already told her she needed to find someplace to stay, and I know she'll be much happier to know someone else has done all the work for her."

His tone was dry as he made that comment, letting me know—as if I didn't already—exactly what his feelings were on the subject of Shelby Howard. I still wasn't terribly thrilled that she'd spent the night at his house, but since I could tell he wanted her out of there as soon as possible, I wasn't going to dwell on that unwelcome fact.

I said, "Well, you'd better text her and let her know what's going on, just so she doesn't book a room on her own."

Noah's mouth quirked. "I kind of doubt it, but you're right."

He reached into his pocket and got out his cell phone. Just as he began typing the message, my own phone—which was still in my hand—rang.

I looked down at the screen, worried it might be Hannah calling me back to tell me she couldn't let Shelby have the cottage after all.

But no, I didn't recognize the number, or the area code. A little puzzled, I touched the screen to accept the call and then put my phone to my ear.

"Charity Hughes...can I help you?"

An older woman's voice, strong, almost imperious. "Well, I certainly hope so," she replied. "Because Cinny has been driving me batty lately!"

"'Cinny'?" I repeated in cautious tones. A quick glance from under my eyelashes told me Noah was absorbed in typing out his text message, but since he was sitting only a few feet away, it wasn't as though he couldn't hear everything I was saying.

"My cat," the woman said, as if that should have been patently obvious. "My familiar," she added, just in case I was so dense I couldn't figure out why someone would be calling me about their cat.

Because that was my one truly unusual witchy gift. My spell-casting abilities were pretty average, but I had the singular talent—one that hadn't appeared for more than a hundred years, according to Grace Bowersby, a local witch who specialized in the history of our kind—of being able to talk to other witches' familiars. Over the years, the witch community had decided that because I could speak to familiars, then I was the perfect person to reach out to for help in case any problems arose.

In fact, that was how I'd first met Noah. He'd bought one of the local vets' practices after the man retired, and I'd had to bring in a hamster who'd thought it was a good idea to go adventuring in my yard, and who'd broken one of her tiny legs. Noah had patched up Lolly just fine...and I'd gotten a chance to look into the vet's piercing blue eyes and fall pretty much instantly in lust.

Anyway, since Noah knew I "fostered" animals...that had seemed the simplest way to describe the parade of familiars that came and went from my property...I knew it was mostly safe to hold this conversation in front of him.

Well, as long as I watched every single word I said.

"Got it," I said. "What seems to be the problem?"

"I'd rather not talk about it on the phone," the

woman replied at once. "Can I bring Cinny over tonight?"

Oh, no way. Not when Noah and I had just patched things up and maybe would try to make up for the dinner we'd missed the night before.

Assuming we got Shelby safely settled at the cottage, that is.

"Tomorrow would be better," I said quickly, which was only the truth. That way, taking in the cat wouldn't wreak havoc on my Sunday night, whatever Noah and I ended up doing, and because my shop would be closed on Monday, that would give me the entire day to get "Cinny" settled at the house.

That suggestion earned me a sniff. However, it seemed the woman was desperate enough to have me troubleshoot what was going on with her familiar that she didn't want to risk antagonizing me, because she only said in ungracious tones, "I suppose that will have to work. I assume ten o'clock will be all right?"

"That would be fine," I replied. "Is Cinny okay with dogs?"

"She is a very agreeable cat...most of the time," the woman said. "I'm sure she won't have a problem with a dog."

"Then I'll see you tomorrow."

The woman—who'd never provided her name —ended the call there, and I guessed that was that.

I slid my phone back in my pocket and looked up to see Noah watching me, a faint smile on his lips.

"Another foster?" he asked, and I nodded.

"She's bringing her cat over tomorrow morning," I said.

"Good," Noah responded, and I lifted an eyebrow.

"'Good'?" I echoed.

"Yes," he said. "Because as soon as I get Shelby settled at the cottage, I'm taking you out to dinner."

Most of the time, I didn't like people telling me what they were going to do so flatly, without leaving any openings for discussion. This time around, though, I was just fine with Noah's pronouncement.

"Sounds like a plan," I said.

Chapter 2

Sweet Cinnamon

I was up fairly early the next day, more out of habit than because I needed to do much to get ready for my meeting with "Cinny's" mysterious mistress. The night before, Noah had excused himself for an hour so he could get Shelby settled at the cottage, but after that, we'd had a late dinner at a local seafood restaurant, where we dined on fish and chips and talked resolutely about ordinary things, like other local food faves and places to go to have fun. He mentioned that a friend had a sailboat and had offered to take us out on the ocean sometime, which sounded like a lot of fun. Even though Salem was situated right on the Atlantic coast, I didn't get many chances to go sailing.

And no, it wasn't because, as a witch, I was afraid of water. That was an old wives' tale, nothing more. No, it was more that I didn't know anyone who owned a boat, and even if I had known someone like that, I didn't have a lot of free time for that sort of thing.

I had no idea whether Shelby had made a rumpus about staying at the cottage, or whether she'd realized she'd ended up in a much better situation than she deserved and so needed to keep her mouth shut. Noah didn't mention her at all during our dinner, and I took the cue from him and made sure to avoid the subject as well.

All the same, I had to admit I was curious.

It seemed I'd have to stay that way, because although I'd gotten a text from Noah a little before ten telling me he'd had a great time the night before and that he was open for lunch if my "foster" meeting didn't run too long, he hadn't said a single word about whether he'd heard from his ex this morning or not.

Which was fine. It definitely didn't take a rocket scientist to figure out he was having as little to do with Shelby as possible, which meant the two of us could go full steam ahead.

Whatever that might turn out to be.

In the meantime, though, I'd tidied up the house—the peremptory tone of the woman dropping off her cat told me she didn't seem like the kind of person who'd tolerate a mess—and put on a black eyelet summer dress, again because I thought it was probably a smart idea to make a good first impression. And I'd also asked Milo if he was okay with us having a visitor for a few days, maybe as long as a week, depending on what was going on with "Cinny."

"I like cats," he replied at once, which was pretty much what I'd expected him to say. Milo was a very easygoing dog, and besides, relationships between familiars weren't the same thing as interactions between ordinary animals. They all had their own personalities, of course, but they were also smart and intuitive, and understood they were different from the animals who hadn't been lucky enough to connect with a witch of their own.

"Good," I said. "It sounds like this kitty is pretty mellow, so the two of you should get along just fine."

We didn't have any time for further conversation, however, because a sharp knock came at the front door, one I hurried to answer. Standing on the front porch was a woman who looked like she was probably in her mid-sixties, with salt-and-pepper hair pulled back into a wide silver clip and narrowed dark eyes. Like me, she wore a black dress, but hers had elbow sleeves and a slim skirt, unlike my lighthearted sleeveless frock with its full skirt.

"I am Doris Dalrymple," she announced, and

nodded down at the cat carrier she held. "And this is Cinnamon."

An orange tabby cat poked her nose against the wire grate at the front of the carrier and looked up at me with curious green eyes. I knew the cat was female because Doris had referred to her as "she" on the phone, but I was surprised to see she was a ginger cat. Female gingers were fairly rare, although not unheard-of.

"Come in," I said, and stepped out of the way so the two could enter the house.

Milo was sitting on the rug in the living room, and eyed the newcomer curiously. However, he didn't say anything, mostly because he knew that, while I would be able to understand him, any words that came out of his mouth would only have sounded like barks and growls to our visitor, since she wasn't his mistress.

"Some tea?" I asked politely. "I have Earl Grey, or—"

"No, thank you," Doris cut in, her tone just this side of rude. "I have a meeting I need to attend after this. I only wanted to drop off Cinny."

Fine, then. The woman definitely wasn't anyone I'd want to hang out with, but I still needed to know a few things before I sent her on her way.

"Well, go ahead and let her out of the carrier," I said. Maybe I sounded a bit arch, but that was probably because I was proud of myself for not telling Doris she needed to learn some manners. I also had to remember that a witch never brought her familiar to me unless she was feeling desperate, which meant I needed to be a little more understanding of her current plight...whatever it turned out to be. "She's going to have the run of the house while she's here, so she might as well get acquainted with the place."

Doris didn't respond directly, but she did lean down so she could undo the latch on the carrier and free Cinny. At once, the cat emerged and went straight over to Milo. His tail wagged, and the two of them touched noses, as if to show Doris that they were going to get along just fine and she had nothing to worry about.

In fact, her thin mouth softened ever so slightly, and she released a breath. "Well, that does seem like a very well-behaved dog."

"He is," I agreed, although I'd already decided not to go into explanations about how I'd inherited him when his former mistress was murdered. The story had probably already run through large portions of the witch community, but even if Doris hadn't heard it yet, I didn't think it was anything she needed to know.

On the other hand, there was plenty I needed to know about Cinnamon.

"So...why do you need me to help with Cinny?" I asked.

Immediately, Doris's mouth tightened again. "We've been having a disagreement," she said.

"About...?" I probed.

Doris crossed her arms. Although she was wearing a silver ring set with a bright green stone on the middle finger of her right hand—I didn't think it was an emerald, but I didn't know what else it might have been—her left hand was conspicuously bare, telling me she was most likely single.

Which wasn't so strange. Lots of witches... including my mother...never married. Being single seemed to have made Doris a lot crabbier than my mother, though.

Or maybe she was just flummoxed by this "disagreement" with her cat.

After a long pause, Doris said, "She wants to have a family."

I blinked. "She what?"

"She wants to have kittens," Doris replied, now sounding more irritated than ever. "I told her that was impossible, of course."

"Of course," I murmured.

On the surface, it really was impossible. Familiars never had offspring. I didn't know whether that was because the same genetic quirk that turned them into familiars also rendered them sterile, or whether it was simply that their connection to their witches...and the correspondingly extended lifespans they enjoyed as a result...

made it so that having a family just wasn't practical.

Either way, I could see why Doris had been baffled by her familiar's unusual request.

I had to admit I was feeling equally perplexed. Did Doris expect me to talk Cinnamon down from her unorthodox desire to have kittens? If that was the case, I didn't know how much help I would be.

But I'd already agreed to take the cat, so I couldn't exactly back out now.

"Well, I'll see what I can do," I said, which was my standard line when confronted by a problem with a familiar that I wasn't quite sure how to solve. "Let me have her for a week, and I'll try to get this worked out."

I didn't add, *one way or another,* even though that was how I finished the sentence in my mind.

Unlike Darla Fitzgerald, Milo's former mistress, Doris didn't even blink at the proposed timeframe. "That will work," she said crisply. A snap of her fingers, and a bag of Science Diet promptly appeared in her hand. "This should be plenty for a week, but just let me know if you need any more."

Feeling a little dazed, I took the bag from Doris. No, it wasn't impossible for a witch to make things materialize out of thin air, but I'd never been very good at that kind of magic. "Treats?" I said weakly.

Another snap of her fingers, and she gave me a

bag of salmon treats. "This should do it," she said. "But I need to be going, or I'll be late."

And she promptly disappeared, leaving me alone with Milo and Cinnamon.

Maybe my chin wagged a little. Witches generally got around on brooms—or by the much more prosaic means of a car or SUV—and I'd never in my life seen a person dematerialize like that. It wasn't strictly impossible, but again, it wasn't the sort of thing most witches could do, either.

Clearly, Doris was a very powerful witch, someone who was used to getting her own way.

No wonder she was irritated with Cinnamon.

"Well," I said cheerfully as I went over to the dining room table and set down the bags of food and treats, "let's all go outside and get acquainted with each other."

That Monday was just as lovely as the day that had preceded it, so it wasn't any hardship to head out to the garden, with Milo and Cinny following me. As far as I could tell, the cat and dog were going to get along famously, which meant at least I wouldn't have to worry about the two of them squabbling.

The three of us sat in the shade of a large oak tree just past the herb garden, where the air was rich with the scent of sea salt and the subtler aromas of rosemary and basil and thyme as it grew beneath the warm late-spring sun. Milo immediately lay down, chin on his paws, nose twitching as he took in all the various interesting smells.

Cinnamon, on the other hand, sat on her haunches, bushy tail curled around her paws, and watched me with interested bright green eyes. "Are you going to try to talk me out of having kittens?" she asked. Like most cats, she had an almost languid voice, one that sounded as if it couldn't be terribly bothered by much of anything.

"Not necessarily," I said, which seemed like a safe enough reply. "I guess I just want to know how you decided that you wanted to have a litter. I've talked with lots of familiars, but you're the first one who's ever told me she wants a family."

The cat's tail flicked ever so slightly, although I got the impression she wasn't annoyed, and instead was only giving herself the time to think over my question. When she spoke, her tone was thoughtful.

"I suppose it's something that's been on my mind for a long time," she said at length. "I would see ordinary cats with their kittens, and wonder why I couldn't have any. The first time I talked to Doris about it, I wasn't even necessarily saying that I wanted a litter, only asking why I'd never seen a familiar with children of their own. But she still got angry with me and told me I shouldn't ask ridiculous questions."

Although I didn't know the woman very well, that sounded exactly like something Ms. Dalrymple would say. Maybe in Doris's mind, the very act of asking such a question might have felt like a kind of betrayal. After all, familiars had been part of witches' lives for hundreds of years, possibly millennia, and in all that time, they'd appeared to be perfectly happy to be their mistress's companions and nothing more.

It sounded to me as though I needed to get Grace Bowersby on the case. She was Salem's unofficial witch historian, and if she didn't have the answer as to why familiars never had families of their own, then I doubted anyone else would.

"Well, I don't think it's ridiculous," I said gently. "Unprecedented, maybe, but not ridiculous. And you've definitely made me wonder why familiars don't have families."

Those words made Cinny sit up a little straighter, and a soft purr began to sound in her throat. Clearly, she wasn't used to someone taking her wants and needs seriously.

True, familiars existed to assist their witches and not the other way around, but most of the time, the connection was a close and loving one. Because of my work with familiars who were acting out in some way, I saw a lot of dysfunctional relationships, but that definitely wasn't the norm. Fewer than one in ten witches even had an animal companion—I didn't, or at least, I didn't have one until Milo came into my life—and probably only five percent of witches with familiars even needed to reach out to me for help. Most of them had been confused and worried...with a few notable exceptions. Doris Dalrymple's outright hostility was a little confounding.

But even though I didn't know much about the woman, I got the definite impression that she was used to having her own way, so dealing with a familiar who'd suddenly announced she wanted a family—and therefore would no longer be at Doris's beck and call—had probably thrown her for a real loop.

Whether I'd be able to get all this sorted out in a week, I had no idea. And I had to admit deep down that I wasn't thrilled to have Doris and Cinny's relationship woes thrown in my lap when I had problems of my own to deal with.

Or maybe not. I definitely wasn't happy to have Shelby Howard in town just as Noah's and my relationship was getting started, but at least he'd made it abundantly clear that he also wasn't exactly thrilled to be dealing with her, either. With any luck, she'd spend a couple of days brooding alone in Hannah Owen's cottage, realize she'd made a huge mistake in splitting from her current fiancé, and would go running back to Boston so she could patch things up. Then Noah and I could continue to let our relationship progress and see what happened.

No harm, no foul.

Because I'd been silent for a moment, Cinny must have thought she needed to speak up. "You don't think I'm crazy, do you?"

"Of course not," I said firmly. "There's absolutely nothing wrong with wanting something different for yourself. And I'll be the first person to tell Doris that, if I need to." I pushed myself up from the grass and added, "But let's go inside so you can explore the house."

The cat seemed amenable to that idea, and the two of us headed for the back door. Milo, on the other hand, appeared perfectly content to keep lying there in the shade of the oak tree for a while longer, because he didn't stir.

Cinny had only begun to poke around the kitchen when my phone buzzed in my skirt pocket. I pulled it out to see a text from Noah.

> Jared's taking the boat out at two. Are you free?

It was only a little after eleven, and I didn't have much on the docket today beyond gathering some more herbs from the garden and making sure Cinny got acclimated to her new environment. I looked over at the cat where she was sniffing at Milo's dog bowls.

"A friend wants me to go sailing with him this afternoon," I said. "Do you mind if I go out for a few hours?"

"Of course not," Cinnamon replied promptly. "I'll have Milo to keep me company. Just because Doris dropped me off here, it doesn't mean I expect you to be home all the time."

Which was a good thing, considering that I'd have to be back at the shop for a normal workday tomorrow. True, in an emergency I could get my assistant, Sage Halloran, to cover for me, but since I'd missed a lot of work while dealing with Darla Fitzgerald's murder and Milo's dognapping, I really didn't want to pull a disappearing act again so soon.

"Thanks, Cin," I said. "It probably won't be for too long...a couple of hours or so."

I didn't add that Noah might want to take me out for drinks afterward, or that he might want me to come over for takeout or something. That's about all I could have managed, since I definitely hadn't planned to make dinner tonight. Anyway, because I didn't know for sure how the rest of the day was going to shape up, I figured it was better not to mention too many hypotheticals.

What I definitely needed to do before I headed out, though, was talk to Grace Bowersby and get her on the case as well. Maybe she'd be able to offer some insights. At the very least, she'd be the best person to start doing some serious research on the subject of familiar families.

The good thing, though, was that Cinny didn't seem to have any problem with being left alone, for which I was definitely grateful. I'd had to babysit familiars in the past who had some serious separation anxiety and who didn't want to be left by themselves for even a few minutes, and that had been stressful...to say the least.

Right now, though, I needed to figure out what to wear. My pretty black eyelet dress had been just fine for my meeting with Doris Dalrymple, but it definitely wasn't appropriate for a boat excursion. Probably one of my few colored tops and some jeans and sneakers would do the trick.

And with Cinny appearing to be very low-maintenance and Shelby Howard safely stashed in Hannah's apartment, it definitely looked like smooth sailing ahead.

Chapter 3

Choppy Waters

"It's great, isn't it?" Noah asked, eyes looking bluer than ever behind the sunglasses he'd donned to shield himself from the glare of the water all around us and the sun above.

I nodded, even as I reached into a pocket of my jeans to get the scrunchie I'd stowed there earlier, guessing I was going to need it as soon as we were out on the open water. Sure enough, the wind off the Atlantic was brisk and had started blowing my wavy red locks around my face even as Noah's friend Jared guided his thirty-foot sailboat out of the harbor.

"Perfect," I replied with a smile.

And it was. I had to admit there was something wild and free about being out on the water, about leaving Salem and all my worries aside. True, I had Grace working on the conundrum of a cat familiar wanting a family, and it seemed as though Shelby was safely settled at Hannah's cottage and therefore out of our hair, but still, being on the boat with Noah—and with Jared and Jared's wife Kathy— felt like I was off in another world somewhere, a place where I could simply think about how good it felt to be alive.

The two of us stood near the cockpit, safely out of Jared and Kathy's way. They'd explained that they needed to guide the boat to catch the prevailing winds and would be performing some complicated tacking maneuvers until we were heading southeast along the shoreline, so Noah and I had taken shelter in a spot where we wouldn't have to risk getting hit in the head with a flapping sail.

"How long have you known Jared?" I asked, since the two men appeared pretty easy and comfortable with one another, which seemed to indicate a longstanding friendship.

"I met him a month or so after I moved to Salem," Noah replied. Kathy had thoughtfully provided bottles of Marblehead beer as we were heading out of the harbor, and he took a sip of the one he held. "His golden retriever stepped on some glass and needed his paw stitched up. We just sort of hit it off, and he and Kathy invited me over for a barbecue. I've been over to their place for dinner a bunch of times—I think Kathy was worried about me living off takeout and frozen dinners."

"Is that what you do?" I asked, amused. Despite my kitchen-witchy skills in making healing potions and such, I actually wasn't a huge cook. I ate takeout probably more than I should, although I would occasionally get overcome with guilt at being so extravagant and make soup or a batch of chili, something I could eat off and on for a week.

Noah grinned. Out there in the bright sunlight, the flash of his white teeth was almost blinding...and his clear blue eyes seemed to scintillate as well, picking up the color of the sky, although the ocean itself was a shifting gray-green.

I blinked, and hoped he hadn't noticed me staring.

"Mostly," he said. "During the summer, I'll throw stuff on the grill when I have a chance, but that's about it. Cooking isn't my thing."

"Mine, either," I responded, figuring I might as well get that admission out of the way. I didn't know exactly where things were going to end up with Noah, but I didn't want him to think I was a kitchen goddess or anything close to that. The last thing I needed was for him to be disappointed somewhere down the line when I confessed I really wasn't up to cooking a sit-down Thanksgiving dinner for twelve, or whatever.

"Then I guess we should both be glad there are

so many good restaurants in Salem," Noah said without missing a beat.

His mouth was still quirked at the corner, telling me he wasn't too worried that I wasn't the latest incarnation of Julia Child.

But I was glad he had his own circle of friends in Salem. Obviously, it hadn't overlapped with mine, since I didn't recall ever seeing Jared or Kathy before today.

Then again, even though Salem wasn't a bustling metropolis or anything, it was a large enough town, with a population of almost 45,000 people, which meant it would be nearly impossible to know everyone who lived there. Also, since Noah's friends appeared to be year-'round residents—he'd told me on the drive over that Jared was an orthodontist and Kathy his office manager—I had a feeling they were like a lot of people who lived in travel destinations, and worked fairly hard to avoid the more touristy areas of town.

Since Full Moon Apothecary was located on Essex Street, one of Salem's most popular tourist spots, I wasn't too surprised that I hadn't seen either one of them there.

Their tacking maneuver apparently complete and the boat now on the sailing version of autopilot— it looked as though we were traveling pretty much due south along the shoreline—Kathy and Jared came up to meet Noah and me at the bow. We drank beer and talked about the weather, and made plans to go out to eat after we got back to the harbor.

It was all utterly, refreshingly normal. True, I experienced my usual pang at realizing I had to keep a huge part of my life secret from these people, but for now, I did my best to put those feelings away and remind myself I needed to relax and live in the moment.

However long that lasted.

Whether or not Noah counted it as a "real" date, since we hadn't been alone, I didn't know for sure. However, his kiss after he dropped me off at home was definitely a bit more passionate than the ones we'd previously shared, making me think he believed our relationship had progressed another step.

I thought it had, too. He'd introduced me to a couple who appeared to be some of his closest friends in Salem, and I doubted he would have done that if he'd thought we didn't have any kind of a future together.

That realization didn't reassure me as much as it might have, however. It was one thing to have fun in the sun with Noah—or even have him help me look for a kidnapped dog—and something else entirely to confess to him that I was a witch, that I came from a long line of witches and there was, in fact, an entire witchy community that existed just below the surface of the everyday world.

How would he even react to that kind of revelation? Yes, I knew witches here in Salem who'd had long and happy marriages, but there were others, like my mother, who'd never met their soulmate and therefore had been forced to keep those secrets hidden.

And since even my short acquaintance with Noah had told me he was a practical, down-to-earth person—like me—I honestly had no idea what he would say even if I did manage to work up the nerve to tell him I wasn't your ordinary garden-variety apothecary shop owner.

Well, those revelations would come a long time from now, if ever. He hadn't said anything about Shelby when he dropped me off, so either she hadn't tried to contact him at all today, or even if she had, he'd decided it wasn't worth mentioning.

Whereas I'd missed two calls from Grace Bowersby, since I'd muted my phone so it wouldn't interrupt my evening out.

After checking on Milo and Cinny—they were curled up against each other on the hearth rug, looking too cute to be believed—I got out my phone so I could listen to Grace's message. There was only the one, even though I had two missed calls. From what I could tell, she'd hung up the first time without leaving a voicemail, but then had decided to call back when it seemed clear I wasn't picking up, for whatever reason.

"I looked through everything I could find," she said in her message. "As far as I can tell, familiars have never had offspring, or even any desire to have families. It seems as though the magic that binds them to their witches is enough to satisfy the need to have a family of their own. But I'll keep looking. Still, it seems very unusual that this cat you're looking after would develop the urge to reproduce, especially since you made it sound as though she's been with her mistress for a long time."

A very long time, considering that Doris Dalrymple looked as though she was at least in her early sixties, maybe more. Witches tended to age well, partly because we had access to handy spells that helped with sagging skin and graying hair, and partly because it seemed as if the magic we carried within us somehow helped to slow the aging process.

Anyway, familiars generally came to their witches when they were little girls of around ten or so, which meant Cinnamon must have been Doris's companion for at least five decades. Familiars didn't age at all, although they almost always passed as soon as their witches left this plane of existence. Milo was a huge exception to that rule, and the only reason I'd been able to come up with as to why he hadn't died when Darla Fitzgerald was murdered was that the connection between the two of them hadn't been very strong.

Grace ended her voicemail with a promise to call me back if she found anything more useful. I set the phone down on the coffee table, and the small sound it made apparently was enough to wake up the two animals.

Milo blinked at me with sleepy eyes and said, "Did you have a good time?"

"I did," I said, and smiled as Cinny got up and stretched, her tail waving languidly at the same time. "It looks like you two had a quiet evening."

"Yes, it was quiet," Cinnamon replied. "But it was nice having Milo here with me. He's much more relaxed than Doris."

Yes, I could see that. Cocker spaniels tended to be fairly mellow dogs; it wasn't as though I'd left Cinny here with a hyperactive Jack Russell terrier or a rambunctious beagle. And even though I didn't know Doris very well, I could already tell she was wound just a little too tight.

"Did you both eat?" I asked next, and the cat and dog nodded in unison.

Clearly, even their brief acquaintance had been enough for them to start picking up on one another's rhythms.

Trying not to smile, I said, "Well, that's good. Milo do you need to go outside?"

At once, he was on his feet, tail wagging. "Yes, please."

I let him outside. Yes, I'd installed a dog door for him, so if he really needed to go without me there, he could, but I think he liked the ritual of having a human open the back door for him. Cinnamon didn't need to worry about such things, since I'd already set up a litter box for her in the laundry room. Now that we were alone, though, I thought it safe to ask her a few questions.

"Cinny, do you remember when you first starting thinking about having kittens?"

The cat was quiet for a moment as she considered my question. "Probably a couple of months ago. One of Doris's neighbors down the street has a big Himalayan, and she had a litter of six kittens. They were adorable, like little puffballs."

I could imagine. "That was the first time you'd ever seen kittens?"

"No, but they were definitely the prettiest," Cinny replied. Then she paused, as if doing her best to ponder her reaction to the neighbor's kittens. "Do you think it's because of that?"

"I don't know," I said honestly. "I suppose it's possible. Or maybe you'd been having this feeling for a while, and seeing the kittens just brought it out that much more."

Cinny's soft orange head tilted to one side. "I really don't want to think I'm that shallow."

Once again, I had to smother a smile. "Oh, I think it's more than that," I assured her. "And you shouldn't feel bad for wanting a family."

That comment got me a wrinkle of her little pink nose. "That's not how Doris looks at it."

"Well, I'm not Doris."

Cinny made a little hissing sound that I knew was the cat equivalent of a snicker. "No, you're not. You're nice."

I raised an eyebrow. "You shouldn't really talk about your mistress like that."

A sigh, followed by, "Oh, I know. And she actually always has been very kind to me—gets me the best treats and scratching posts, and buys me fluffy beds and plenty of catnip and mouse toys."

Maybe I needed to revise my opinion of Doris Dalrymple a bit. It definitely sounded as though she did whatever she could to pamper her pet, behavior that was a far cry from the neglectful environment Milo had come from. No, Darla Fitzgerald hadn't abused the dog, but everything I'd heard and seen had made it seem as if she did the bare minimum to give him a comfortable life.

"But it wasn't enough," I said slowly, and Cinny's tail flicked from side to side.

"It was for a long time," she said. "But it isn't now."

* * *

Later that night as I was getting ready to go to sleep —and after both Milo and Cinnamon had curled up around each other on the afghan that was spread across the foot of my bed—I got a text from Noah.

> Takeout at my place tomorrow night?

I resisted the urge to hug the phone like some teenager who'd just gotten a message from her crush. At the same time, though, I couldn't help thinking about Shelby Howard. What if she decided to turn up while I was over at Noah's house?

> Maybe mine would be safer.

His response came back almost immediately.

> No, it's fine. If Shelby shows up & sees you there, maybe it'll help drive it home that I've moved on.

That he was willing to state such a thing so baldly told me he viewed our nascent relationship as something serious, even though we'd only been seeing each other for a few days. I couldn't help being encouraged by that, even if the more cautious side of my nature was warning me maybe we should be taking it slow.

But I also wasn't going to argue with meeting at his house. Like he'd said, if Shelby made the mistake of appearing where she hadn't been invited, she might learn a few truths she really didn't want to acknowledge.

Okay, see you then. What time?

7 okay?

It's perfect.

We ended the convo there, and I set my phone down on the nightstand.

Maybe things were progressing faster than I'd expected, but I was okay with that.

More than okay, really.

* * *

The next day I had to go to work, but Milo and Cinny stayed at home after assuring me they'd be much happier there.

"After all, here I can go outside whenever I want," Milo had pointed out. "It's much more interesting than having to stay cooped up in the back of the shop all day."

Because that was the truth—and because it was

pretty obvious to me that he and Cinny were already fast friends, and would be able to keep themselves amused while I was at the store—I didn't feel too bad about leaving them home. Yes, I experienced the slightest twinge as I backed out of the driveway and realized I wouldn't see them again until the end of the day, but I told myself it would be all right. The man who'd kidnapped Milo was dead, and it didn't seem as if there was anyone else out there who meant the dog harm...or Cinny, either. No, her issue involved a difference of opinion with her mistress and nothing more, which meant she should be perfectly safe as well.

Because it was the Tuesday after a holiday weekend, things were mostly quiet at the shop. Yes, we had tourists come and go, people who'd extended their Memorial Day vacation past the holiday itself, but it was nothing like the mobs who'd descended only a few days earlier.

That gave me some time to get Sage, my assistant, up to speed about how I already had a new familiar I was working with.

"But she's really low-maintenance," I said. "So I don't think having her at the house is going to interfere with work."

Sage gave a careless lift of her shoulders. She was seven years younger than I, just a little past twenty-two, and not a lot seemed to rile her, a good trait to possess when working with the public.

Not that she planned to make a career of working in an apothecary shop. So far, she hadn't really indicated what she wanted to do with her life, but she was a very good assistant, and I was glad to have her for as long as she was willing to hang around.

"Even if you do need to leave to take care of the cat," Sage told me, "I can cover for you here. I doubt it's going to be too busy this week."

Probably not. In other parts of the country, kids were already getting out of school, but in Salem and the area that surrounded it, the summer break wouldn't start until mid-June. That meant we probably had a few quiet weeks before the next influx, something I was just fine with. Yes, I needed the shop to support itself, but I didn't want to work myself to death to make that happen.

"Well, I doubt it'll come to that," I replied, and Sage just nodded. Because it was such a warm day today, she had her sleek brown hair pinned up in a knot at the back of her neck, emphasizing the slender lines of her neck and showcasing her big hazel eyes. In fact, I'd noticed how a boy in the last group who'd come in—clearly a family—had kept staring at her, even though I guessed she was probably four or five years older than he was.

It wasn't the first time she'd been stared at, and I doubted it would be the last.

And actually, the day turned out to be busier

than either of us had expected, which was just fine by me. It made the time pass that much more quickly, and soon enough, five o'clock rolled around, and we could lock up and head our separate ways.

When I got home, it was to find Milo and Cinnamon lying on the sofa, watching *Animal Planet*.

"Who gave you the remote?" I joked.

"Oh, I learned how to use it at my house," Cinny replied, looking unperturbed. "It's a fun way to pass the time."

"I suppose it is," I said. "And that's good, because I'm going over to Noah's for dinner tonight."

Neither of the animals looked too upset by that announcement, although Milo said, "Will you be bringing home any table scraps?"

"If there are leftovers, I'll try to bring some back," I assured him, accompanying my promise with a pat on the head.

This assurance seemed to be all he needed, because he gave me a doggy smile and then headed out to the backyard, with Cinnamon tagging along behind him. I had to admit that knowing they got along so well together made me feel a lot less guilty about leaving them home alone tonight.

Especially since they seemed just fine with amusing themselves by watching cable TV.

* * *

I hadn't heard anything else from Grace, but I told myself that was fine. Doris had given me a week to work with Cinnamon, so we had plenty of time to try getting to the bottom of the cat's desire for a family. It did sound as if it was something that had come on recently, not a wish she'd been hiding from her mistress for years and years.

But why? Was it some kind of spell?

I supposed that was remotely possible. Witches used spells for anything and everything, whether it was getting their bread to rise properly or making sure a lottery ticket would hand them an extra ten or fifteen thousand dollars. We worked prosperity enchantments all the time, although winning really big—like a million dollars or more—was frowned upon, just because that sort of thing tended to attract too much attention.

However, even if another witch had cast a spell to make Cinnamon wish for a litter of kittens, I couldn't really understand why she would want to do such a thing. Yes, familiars were a big help, could assist a witch in working enchantments in addition to providing companionship and a sounding board, but plenty of witches got along just fine without one. Making Cinny preoccupied with kittens seemed like an odd way to get back at Doris when there were plenty of far less roundabout ways to send a hex in her direction.

Witches didn't like to admit there was ever dissent in our ranks. We preferred to think of ourselves as a unified bloc, even though that wasn't always the case. From time to time, witches could fall into feuds with one another, sometimes over something as simple as a stolen spell or someone poaching another witch's favorite place to gather mandrake root. In general, it wasn't good to have two users of magic flinging random spells at one another, so any time one of these disagreements cropped up, other witches would step in to make sure it got calmed down before the general public noticed anything.

So, I supposed it was possible someone had put a very subtle hex on Cinny, even if I couldn't really understand why.

For now, though, I needed to push those questions aside and enjoy my evening with Noah. It wouldn't be a late one, because we both had to go to work the next day, but we could still have a few fun hours together.

After making sure that both Milo and Cinny had their own dinners waiting for them in their respective bowls and that they both had plenty of fresh water, I headed over to Noah's house. By that time of the evening, Salem's mild rush hour had dissipated, and I could allow myself to enjoy the mellow light as the sun sank to the west...and also bask in the realization that we still had an entire summer in front of us, a summer I hoped I would be able to share with him.

He definitely looked cheerful and relaxed when he let me in, telling me he probably hadn't heard from Shelby that day.

Maybe she really was being serious about examining her life choices.

Noah and I decided on Thai, and popped open a bottle of rosé as we waited in the living room for the Door Dash driver to arrive with our meals.

"How was the shop?" he asked as he poured some wine for me.

"Oh, it was good," I said. "Nothing earth-shattering, which, after last week, was a welcome change."

He grinned. "I get it. And Milo's still doing fine?"

"Getting a little better every day," I replied.

I didn't add that Milo's accelerated recovery from the creature that had attacked him the week before might have had something to do with the gentle healing potions I'd been adding to his water the past couple of days. Noah had done a great job of patching him up, but there was still more going on than met the eye.

"And he's getting along really well with the cat I'm fostering," I continued. A sudden thought struck me, and I asked, "Would you mind taking a look at her sometime this week when you're not too busy?"

Noah's expression sobered. "What's wrong?"

"Oh, nothing," I said hastily. The last thing I wanted was for him to think I'd been ignoring any health conditions Cinny might have...or was possibly angling for more free vet assistance. I realized then that Noah had never sent me a bill for his emergency trip to my house to help with Milo after the attack. An oversight, or did he think he shouldn't charge me for services rendered now that we were seeing each other?

If that was the case, I'd have to disabuse him of such a notion as soon as seemed appropriate. The Hughes witches didn't take handouts.

But because he was watching me with one eyebrow lifted slightly, obviously waiting for me to continue, I went on, "I just wanted you to check her and see if she would be able to have a litter. Her owner would love to have some ginger kittens."

"She's not spayed?"

I shook my head and said quickly, "No, she's always been an indoor cat, and I suppose Ms. Dalrymple never got around to it."

Well, that wasn't exactly the truth. Witches never had to spay their female animal companions because they never went into heat. Normally, that would have implied they were infertile, but I didn't know if the situation was as cut and dried as that.

Either way, I hoped a physical examination by a skilled vet might provide some of the answers I was looking for.

Before Noah could reply to my comment, his phone rang. He sent me an apologetic look and dug his phone out of his pocket, then grimaced.

"It's Shelby."

"Better see what she wants," I said, hoping I didn't sound too annoyed. At least she'd called before our food arrived.

Noah put the phone to his ear. "Shelby, I'm kind of in the middle of—"

He stopped there, slightly exasperated expression turning to one of shock. "He what?"

A long pause while he listened to her reply.

Then he said, "You need to call the police. I—"

I had a feeling she'd cut him off, because he didn't get any further than that. As he listened, his brow furrowed.

At length, he said, "All right. I'll be over as fast as I can. Don't touch anything."

He ended the call and stood up, even as he returned the phone to his pocket.

I rose from the couch as well. "What's going on?"

A helpless lift of his shoulders, and he said, "I'm not totally sure. She was kind of hysterical."

That I could imagine. It wasn't as though I knew the woman well—or at all—but she definitely didn't seem like the most stable person in the world.

The words came out of my mouth before I could stop them. "Need me to come along?"

I'd halfway expected him to say no, but, to my surprise, he released a breath and said, "Sure. I could probably use the moral support."

And that was why we hurried out, me with my phone to my ear so I could cancel our Door Dash order, even as we climbed into Noah's Toyota Tundra. We sped off toward the cottage where Shelby was staying, neither one of us speaking.

My own thoughts were going a mile a minute, though. Noah had mentioned the police. Had someone broken in, maybe tried to assault her? I couldn't imagine that sort of thing happening in quiet Salem, Massachusetts—our crime rate was pretty low—but I supposed a woman on her own staying in a strange place could be kind of a target.

At any rate, we should find out soon enough.

We pulled up to the cottage, a cute white-painted house with dark blue shutters and a welcoming front porch. The windows were shut, and pansies bloomed cheerfully from planters beneath those same windows.

It definitely didn't look as though anyone had

broken in…unless they'd gone into the house from the back.

Noah and I got out of the truck and headed up the front path. Once we reached the door, he knocked, saying, "Shelby? It's Noah."

The door opened almost immediately, and a white-faced Shelby stared out at us. Maybe a blink as she registered my presence, but it seemed she had more important things to worry about, because she stepped out of the way as we entered the cottage, saying, "I didn't do it. You have to believe me—I didn't do it!"

For a second, I couldn't understand what the heck she was talking about. But then my eyes focused on the dim interior of the cottage and made out the limp form of a man lying on the cheerful floral-patterned rug that covered the floor.

There was a sword sticking straight out of his back.

Wild-eyed, Shelby repeated, "I swear I didn't do it!"

Chapter 4

Backstabber

Noah, not quite as shocked as I was, had the presence of mind to close the door behind us—after wrapping his fingers in his untucked shirttail so he wouldn't leave any fingerprints behind.

Voice level, he said, "Is that Trevor?"

Shelby nodded. Once again, her wild blue eyes flicked toward me, but since I'd already decided the smartest thing to do was keep my mouth shut, I didn't say anything. In fact, my hands were shaking. I might have figured out who'd killed Darla Fitzgerald, but I'd never seen her dead body, never been anywhere near the scene of the crime. That I was now standing only a few feet away from a corpse was an unsettling experience, to say the least.

Actually, there wasn't as much gore as I might have expected. The man was lying face down and wore a dark blue shirt. Blood had soaked the fabric around the blade that protruded from his back, but it almost looked as though the sword itself was keeping too much more from flowing out of the wound and pooling on the floor.

In silence, Noah knelt on the floor and placed his index and middle fingers against the dead man's throat. His expression was resigned, as if he already knew he wasn't going to feel a pulse but felt he needed to make the effort anyway. Then he climbed back to his feet and looked over at Shelby.

"What happened?" he asked next, still in that unnaturally calm voice. I had a feeling he was keeping a tight rein on his emotions so he could hold it together and handle the situation as rationally as possible.

Lord knows Shelby wasn't in any condition to do so.

With shaking fingers, she pushed back a few locks of honey-blonde hair, tucking them behind her ears. The last time I'd seen her as she opened the door to Noah's house, she'd appeared calm and breezy, confident in her good looks.

Now she could have stood in for the "final girl" in a horror movie, with her pale face and panicky eyes. The only thing that was missing was blood smears all over her light pink top, but it seemed she'd retained enough presence of mind not to touch her fiancé's corpse.

"I—" She swallowed a breath, then went on, "Trevor called earlier today and said he wanted to talk. I told him there wasn't anything to talk about, but he kept insisting, so I said okay, come on up to the cottage, and I gave him the address."

"What time did he get here?"

"Around three."

Noah and I exchanged a glance. I wasn't exactly what you could call an expert on crime scenes or anything, but it sure looked to me as though Trevor hadn't been dead for very long, that Shelby had grabbed her phone and called Noah just as soon as she thought it was safe.

"So...who did this?" he asked, still keeping his gaze fixed on Shelby. I could tell he didn't want to look at the body on the floor for any longer than absolutely necessary.

"I don't know!" she replied, tone getting wilder. "It all happened so fast."

"Maybe you should sit down," I said, trying to keep my voice gentle, calm.

She flicked me an annoyed glance, and for a moment I thought she was going to protest, was going to tell me she didn't need to sit. However, she apparently decided her knees were wobbly after all, and took a few stumbling steps toward the chintz-covered couch and sort of collapsed on it.

"Where did the sword come from?" Noah inquired next, a reasonable enough question. After all, the cottage was something out of a Laura Ashley catalogue gone wild, with lots of floral prints and whitewashed furniture and cute knick-knacks. It wasn't exactly the kind of place that would have a sword hanging on the wall.

"It—it's Trevor's," Shelby managed.

The words slipped out before I could think. "He brought a *sword* with him?"

She gave an impatient head shake, accompanied by a scornful glance. Even in her currently distraught state, it was pretty clear she didn't have much use for me.

Well, I was here, and although I was thinking it probably would have been better for me to stay at home, there wasn't anything I could do about it now.

"No," she said emphatically. "Swords are his hobby. He fenced in college...he went to Yale."

Of course he did.

Before either Noah or I could say anything in reply, however, she continued. "He's been collecting swords for years. I recognized this one because Trevor had it hanging in his office at work."

"If he didn't bring it with him...." Noah began,

then trailed off, as if he knew he didn't have enough pieces of the story to finish the sentence.

"He didn't," Shelby said, tone just as firm as it had been a moment earlier. "He drove up and brought an overnight bag with him, just in case."

She didn't say in case of what, but the implications of him bringing a suitcase were obvious enough to me. Had he been that confident about getting things with Shelby patched up, or was he the sort of person who didn't take no for an answer?

If that was the case, I could see why he might have enough enemies to end up with a sword sticking out of his back...except for the part where Shelby had sworn up and down that she didn't have anything to do with it.

Her hands gripped one another, restless. I had the idle thought that I'd never seen anyone wringing their hands in real life, and yet here it was.

"Okay," Noah said, still calm. However, his jaw was tense, and I got the feeling what he really wanted to do was whip out his phone and call the police, no matter what Shelby might think about contacting the authorities. But he managed to stay on track, and continued. "So, Trevor came over around three. What happened after that?"

"We talked," she replied. Now that she was sitting down, she didn't seem quite as agitated... well, except for her hands, whose constant motion reminded me of a couple of snakes writhing around each other. "He apologized for being controlling, said he'd made a huge mistake and wanted for us to work things out."

The gossipy side of my brain wanted to know exactly how controlling Trevor had been, what he'd done that was so extreme, it had caused Shelby to break up with him. However, since I barely knew the woman and was currently dating her ex, I figured it was better to remain silent and let her go on with her story.

"All right," Noah responded. "So, you talked the whole time?"

"No," she said. "We went out to get an early dinner, since neither one of us had any lunch and we were hungry. A place called the Mercy Tavern."

A restaurant where Noah and I had planned to go out to eat on several different occasions, only to get stymied each time when some kind of crime-related circumstances got in the way. At any rate, it sounded as though Shelby and Trevor had been in a pretty public place, which meant it shouldn't be too difficult to corroborate that part of her story.

As soon as that thought passed through my brain, I wanted to shake my head at myself. Just because I'd managed to figure out who had killed Darla Fitzgerald, that didn't make me Sherlock Holmes...or even a member of a CSI team. No, as soon as Shelby was done telling her story, we'd call the police, and after that, the matter would be out of our hands.

"We got back from dinner a little before seven," she went on. "We were both thirsty, so I went into the kitchen to get us some glasses of water. Just as I was shutting the refrigerator door, I heard noises from the front room."

"What kind of noises?"

"Banging, shuffling," she replied. "I left the water in the kitchen and hurried out to see what was going on. Trevor was in the living room, wrestling with someone."

"Did you get a good look at them?"

At once, she shook her head. "No. They were wearing all black, and they were wearing some kind of black thing that covered their entire head, too."

Clearly, whoever had assaulted Trevor Miller had come here with murder on their mind, or I doubted they would have gone to such lengths to conceal their identity.

On the other hand, ninjas were kind of in short supply in Salem, Massachusetts, so it seemed possible that one of the neighbors might have seen the intruder going into the house, might have even caught a glimpse of what kind of vehicle they were driving.

Noah was frowning a little, telling me he wasn't thrilled to hear that Shelby hadn't gotten a good look at the murderer's face. However, he asked in that same even, neutral tone, "What happened after that?"

"They were holding Trevor's sword," she said. "They shoved it into his back. I screamed."

You'd think the neighbors would have heard something.

Then again, all the windows were closed, probably because Shelby had locked everything up before she and Trevor headed out to dinner.

"And then?" Noah prompted.

Shelby finally stopped wringing her hands, but only so she could reach up with shaking fingers and push back the lock of hair that had just slipped past her ear. "They came at me and pushed me out of the way, then went running into the kitchen. I suppose they must have gone out through the back door."

And escaped into the backyard, and disappeared. Like a lot of Salem's other older homes, Hannah Owen's cottage backed up onto an alley. For all anyone knew, the murderer had left their car parked back there, waiting to make their getaway. Because the property was a vacation rental, it wasn't as though any of the neighbors would have noticed anything unusual about an unfamiliar vehicle being left behind the cottage.

Noah must have been thinking about the same thing, because his usually friendly mouth was tight, his gaze sober. Still, he asked, "Any signs of forced entry?"

"No," Shelby said, then gave a helpless little lift of her shoulders. "But that's my fault. We were in such a hurry to go out to dinner, I don't think I got the deadbolt to lock properly. It's kind of temperamental."

Well, that was great. No way to tell exactly how the murderer had gotten in, and no way to identify them, thanks to how they'd been covered in black from head to toe.

But I had to give Noah credit for not giving up. He crossed his arms and said, "Okay, you couldn't see the murderer's face, but can you remember if they were particularly tall or short?"

Shelby stared down at her feet, which were covered in a pair of nude-toned ballet flats. "Not really," she replied. "Like I said, it happened really fast. They were taller than me, but I can't remember exactly by how much. They were strong, though," she added hopefully, as if she thought that might be enough of a distinguishing character-istic to help identify Trevor's assailant from among a lineup of other ninja-dressed killers.

Unfortunately, I didn't think the cops asked suspects to bench-press a couple of hundred pounds as a way of establishing their identity.

And honestly, it seemed pretty obvious that the

killer would have to be strong, considering how they'd managed to shove that sword so deep in Trevor's back. I doubted I'd be able to do anything like that, and I liked to think I kept myself in pretty decent shape.

Noah let out a breath, one that was noticeable when contrasted with how calm he'd been during this entire interview. "I'm really sorry this happened to you, Shelby," he said. "And you know I'll be here for you to help you get through this. But we have got to call the police."

"Really?" she repeated, now sounding like a little girl who was disappointed when her parents told her she couldn't get a pony for her birthday.

"Really," Noah said firmly. "They're probably not going to be too thrilled that you called me first, but I'll just try to explain how you were upset and weren't thinking clearly."

Her full mouth turned down slightly at that remark. To my relief, though, she didn't comment, and instead only gave a reluctant nod.

"If you have to."

Noah's gaze met mine for a second, and I allowed myself a very small shrug. Yes, I'd asked a question or two, but this definitely wasn't my call to make.

"All right," he said, and got out his phone.

* * *

"They arrested Shelby?" I asked in astonishment.

After Noah called the police, two detectives and two uniformed officers arrived at the cottage. They asked Noah and me a few curt questions, and, after determining both of us had arrived on the scene after the murder had occurred, had made it pretty clear they wanted to talk to Shelby alone. Because the night had been crazy enough without getting arrested for interfering with an investigation, Noah had driven me home, and promised he would let me know what was happening as soon as he knew anything.

Which was why I was currently on the phone with him, even though it was almost eleven and I really should have been getting ready for bed.

"Yes," he said gloomily. "They said enough of her story didn't add up that they're going to hold her for additional questioning."

"That's crazy," I replied. No, I might not have been Shelby Howard's biggest fan, but even I could tell she couldn't possibly have done anything like this. And if she really had been the one who'd driven that sword into Trevor Miller's back, then she had to be the world's greatest actress.

"It is," Noah agreed. "But at least she retained enough presence of mind to contact her mother's attorney. He'll be here in the morning."

I reflected that was something...even as I

wondered who her mother was that she had a criminal-defense lawyer on speed dial.

But maybe he was just your ordinary run-of-the-mill family lawyer, and was only handling things until Shelby's mother could find someone who specialized in representing defendants in murder cases. That scenario made a lot more sense.

Because, even though I didn't know much about Shelby, I could tell she ran in the kind of circles where using a public defender would have been out of the question.

"So...now what?" I asked. Maybe this wasn't the first time I'd stumbled into a murder case, but when Darla Fitzgerald was killed, the police didn't have any suspects, no one to take into custody. It wasn't until I'd basically handed them Brian Alatorre on a platter that they had any leads at all, and he'd conveniently died in his sleep—thanks to some magical intervention that I still didn't want to examine too closely—before anyone could even begin to mount some kind of defense for him.

"We wait," Noah said. "It's a regular weekday tomorrow, so I'm hoping Shelby will be arraigned early and the judge will allow her bail, considering she doesn't have any kind of a record."

"And if he doesn't?"

"Then she sits in jail until her trial," he replied. "I doubt that's going to happen, though. Luckily, her mother should be able to swing bail unless it's really enormous."

He hadn't said anything about pitching in to help, and I had to admit I felt a little relieved. Maybe I should have been more magnanimous, but since he and Shelby had been broken up for a year and it seemed as though she'd been pretty well out of his life until she reappeared out of nowhere only the day before yesterday, I didn't see why Noah should feel responsible for bailing out his ex-fiancée.

If he could even afford such a thing. I thought his vet business was doing very well, but he still had a mortgage of his own—or pretty expensive rent, if he didn't own his house—and I had no idea how much he'd paid for Dr. Campbell's practice after he retired. In general terms, Noah was probably doing all right for himself, and yet I kind of doubted he had huge chunks of change lying around for bail money.

"Well, that's good," I replied, and paused, not sure what I should say next.

He must have picked up on the hesitation in my tone, because he said quickly, "Well, I just wanted to let you know what was going on. I've got to get to bed, though—I've got surgery first thing tomorrow morning."

I wasn't doing anything quite so important,

but I also knew it was time to get some sleep. "Just let me know if you need anything," I told him.

"I will," he said, then paused. Although I couldn't see his face, I guessed he was smiling right then. "One of these days we'll be able to go on a real date."

"One of these days," I echoed, smiling myself.

We ended the call there, and I headed into the bathroom to brush my teeth and wash my face. Both Milo and Cinny were already curled at the foot of my bed; when I'd gotten home this evening, I'd filled them in on what had happened, and warned that I might have to go help Noah if he asked. Neither one of them had seemed too concerned—after all, they didn't know Shelby, and Cinny had never met Noah at all—but Milo had said he hoped Dr. Noah wasn't too upset by everything that was happening and that it would all work out okay.

But, as Noah himself had pointed out, about all any of us could do now was wait.

* * *

Salem wasn't such a big town that the news hadn't already made the rounds. When Sage came into the shop the next morning, her pretty features were bright with curiosity.

"You can't catch much of a break from these

murder cases, can you?" she said, and I gave her a rueful smile.

"I guess not," I replied. "Although in this case, I just happened to be in the wrong place at the wrong time. None of this has much to do with me."

Sage didn't seem too deterred by my comment, since she said next, "Is it true that you found the guy with a sword sticking out of his back?"

"Yes," I said, even as I reflected that this felt like it was going to be a very long day. "Or at least, Shelby found him first, but he was still that way when Noah and I showed up."

Sage shook her head. "Wild. It's not the kind of thing I ever thought would happen here in sleepy old Salem."

Me neither. Despite its complement of witches, Salem tended to be a quiet sort of place, with nothing all that out of the ordinary happening here. We witches did our best to keep it that way, too, since the last thing we wanted was to draw any attention to ourselves.

Well, attention had been drawn, although I highly doubted the ninja-ish murderer was a witch. For one thing, Shelby had described the killer as being taller than she was, and since she herself was quite tall—probably a good two or three inches more than my own five foot seven—the odds were that whoever had driven that sword into Trevor's back, they were probably male.

And because I'd spotted several news vans headed toward downtown and the police station as I drove to work today, I guessed the murder had been spectacular and unusual enough that it had drawn the attention of the Boston affiliates.

Just doing their jobs, I supposed, although I really hoped none of them had gotten enough details about the scene of the crime to learn that Noah and I had been there. Getting interviewed even on the local news wasn't my idea of maintaining a low profile.

But either the Salem police had remained tight-lipped about the way Noah and I had been at the cottage before they were even called, or the reporters had decided I wasn't worthy of being interviewed, because no one except the usual complement of tourists and local shoppers came into Full Moon Apothecary that day. I didn't hear anything from Noah, either, and that didn't thrill me quite so much. True, he'd already made it sound as if he had a full slate at the clinic, but I still hoped he would have reached out, if only to give me some kind of update on Shelby's status.

Right at the end of the day, though, I got a text from him.

> Shelby made bail and wants to talk to us. Can you come over to my house @ 6?

Not exactly what I'd wanted to hear. Oh, I was glad Shelby had gotten bailed out and wouldn't be stuck in jail for an indeterminate length of time, but on the other hand, I also wasn't too keen to hang out with her.

No, I wanted Noah all to myself.

I allowed the selfish thought to cross my mind, and then banished it to the outer darkness. Whatever Noah and Shelby's history—or his and my future—the poor woman had been through hell during the past twenty-four hours. The least I could do was hear what she wanted to say.

> Sure, I'll come by after work. Need me to bring anything?

> No, just yourself. We'll probably order pizza or something.

I sent him a thumbs-up to indicate I was on board with the plan, then stowed my phone in my purse and went on with closing up the shop.

If nothing else, I had to admit I was kind of curious as to why Shelby had called this meeting.

* * *

For someone who'd spent the night in jail, Shelby was looking pretty decent. It seemed obvious she'd had time to get herself cleaned up before our meeting, because her blonde hair gleamed in the late afternoon light that slanted through the windows of Noah's living room, and she was wearing dark skinny jeans and an embroidered sleeveless blouse that I guessed must have come from an expensive boutique in Boston.

Had she done all this primping at Noah's house? I had to believe the cottage was still a crime scene, so unless she'd found herself a last-minute hotel room, she wouldn't have had anywhere else to go.

I didn't like that particular idea, even as I tried to tell myself I shouldn't be so petty, especially since Noah had been emphatic about no longer harboring any feelings for her.

"Thank you so much for coming over," she told me.

The way she'd said it, she almost made it sound as though this was hers and Noah's house. However, I reminded myself that she'd just been through a terrible ordeal and probably wasn't in any condition to be paying attention to her tone or phrasing.

"It's fine," I replied. "How are you doing?"

"About as well as can be expected," she said.

The three of us were sitting in the living room,

with Shelby on the couch and Noah and I in a pair of armchairs that faced the sofa. It probably would have made more sense for our positions to be reversed, but since she was already seated on the sofa when I arrived, I wasn't going to comment.

Noah had gotten all of us glasses of water, although nobody had touched theirs yet. Personally, I would have preferred something a little stronger than water, but I supposed I could see why he thought it better for us to be clear-headed while having this discussion.

"My mother took care of bail," she went on. "The judge said I had to stay in town, and she and I found another Airbnb so I can be here for as long as I need to."

Well, that answered my questions about where she'd gotten cleaned up. At the same time, though, I wasn't sure I liked the sound of her hanging around Salem very much. True, there was nothing going on between Noah and Shelby, but at the same time, I wasn't sure I wanted them to be in each other's laps all summer, either.

Good thing she'd found another place to stay, though, because I knew Hannah's cottage had only been available for a few days, not the entire summer.

"I'm glad you found a place to land," Noah said. His tone was almost too neutral, and that cheered me up a bit. If he really had been happy about Shelby being here for the duration, he probably would have sounded much peppier.

"Yes, that's one less thing to worry about." She leaned over to pick up her glass of water from the coffee table and took a sip. "The police notified Trevor's family, of course, but I haven't heard anything from them." Her mouth, now perfectly glossed, thinned a little. "I hope they don't think I had anything to do with all this."

"I doubt it," Noah said. "They're probably just in shock right now and trying to figure out what to do next."

To be honest, Shelby didn't look as upset as I'd thought she would be. I supposed it was entirely possible that she'd cried herself out while lying awake in a jail cell, but if that was how she'd spent the previous night, she didn't show any sign of it now—no puffy eyes, makeup and hair flawless. For all I knew, presenting a perfect image to the world was her way of coping with the tragedy that had just intruded on her life, and yet I couldn't help feeling a twinge of unease.

What if she really had killed Trevor and was trying to fool all of us with her story about a ninja-style murderer breaking into her rented cottage? I really didn't want to believe such a thing, but....

Before my mind could wander down any darker paths, Shelby spoke again. "You're probably right. But if they really *do* think I killed Trevor—if anyone at all is thinking such a horrible thing about me—then I need to do whatever I can to clear my name."

She paused there, her gaze fixed on me. I stared back, not sure why she'd just made me the focus of her attention.

"Charity, that's why I need you to figure out who really killed Trevor."

Chapter 5

A Dose of Charity

For a second or two, I could only stare back at Shelby Howard, not sure I'd heard her correctly.

Why in the world would she think I'd be able to track down her fiancé's killer?

Her next words cleared up that particular mystery, however.

"Noah told me how you figured out who killed your dog's former owner," she went on. "So I'm sure you'll be able to help me, too."

Because she was watching me with earnest eyes, I couldn't exactly turn on Noah and demand that he tell me why he'd gone blabbing to Shelby. Also, even though he knew I'd discovered Darla's killer, I hadn't gone into any real details as to how I'd managed to accomplish such a feat.

How could I, when I knew what had really helped me was magic?

"Um...that was pretty much luck," I managed.

Not even a complete lie. If I hadn't had a couple of lucky breaks while trying to find out who'd murdered Darla Fitzgerald, Brian Alatorre would probably still be a free man.

Or creature, or whatever you wanted to call him. I was still having a hard time understanding how magic could twist someone with a Y chromosome into something other, something terrible. It was that awful sex-linked characteristic which had made generations of witches cast spells to make sure they only had daughters, not the awful shape-changing creature Brian had been.

"Oh, I think it was more than that," Noah said. "I mean, it sounded as though the Chicago police were totally stumped, and yet you figured out the mystery."

While under other circumstances I might have enjoyed receiving such praise, right now I just wished Noah would keep his mouth shut. Of course I didn't enjoy the idea of an innocent person going to prison, but at the same time, I wasn't exactly eager to be giving his former fiancée any assistance. Maybe she'd conveniently forgotten how she'd introduced herself as his current fiancée when I went over to his house a few days ago, but I sure as hell hadn't.

That was just me being petty, though. Even if I didn't like her style...even though I thought she fit the "crazy ex" stereotype pretty damn perfectly...I knew I couldn't stand by and let her take the fall for something she hadn't done.

Besides, if I actually managed to figure out who had killed Trevor Miller, that meant she'd be out of my hair that much sooner. Maybe not the most altruistic reason for agreeing to take on the case, but I wouldn't let myself worry about that.

After all, I was a witch, not an angel.

"I don't know how much I can do," I said slowly. "I mean, I'm no Veronica Mars or anything. But of course I'll help."

Shelby beamed at me, relief clear in every plane of her face, and Noah relaxed against the back of the chair where he sat, the shift in his posture telling me he was also glad that I hadn't refused her request. "You have no idea how much I appreciate you doing this for me," she said. "If there's any way I can repay you, just let me know."

"No payment required," I replied at once, even while those words rankled more than they probably should. Had she just assumed I needed the cash? I could already tell she—or her family—had money, but that didn't make me a charity case.

No pun intended.

I added, "I just hate the idea of anyone going to

jail for something they didn't even do. But I also hope you've retained a good attorney."

Her megawatt smile didn't even flicker. "Oh, I've got the best," she told me. "He said the police don't have anything except circumstantial evidence, and also, there was no reason for me to have murdered Trevor in the first place."

Except the part where you two were supposedly estranged, I thought, although I didn't say anything out loud. From what I could tell, it seemed as if the two of them had been working out whatever had caused the rift in the first place, so "estranged" probably wasn't even the right way to describe the current state of their relationship.

Or at least, where their relationship had been right before Trevor's untimely death.

"That's good to hear," Noah said. He'd been quiet during the previous exchange, probably deciding he should stay out of the way until Shelby and I had hammered out some kind of agreement. "And I hope you continue to take his advice."

"I will," Shelby replied. "But I'm hoping Charity will get this figured out before we get anywhere close to a trial."

No pressure, I thought. But, considering how long it could take before a case like this was even decided by a jury, I could see why she was hoping I'd get the murder solved lickety-split. After all, it had taken me less than a week to track down Brian

Alatorre, but there had been some special circumstances involved.

"We'll just have to see," I said, which was about all I could commit to right then. Mostly, I just wanted to get out of there so I could start determining how I would even go about doing such a thing.

To my infinite relief, Shelby's phone rang from inside her purse, which had been sitting next to her on the sofa. The briefest flash of irritation flitted across her features, but she reached inside anyway and pulled it out.

"My mom," she said briefly as she glanced down at the screen, then went ahead and put the iPhone to her ear. "Yes, I'm still at Noah's," she went on, obviously speaking to her mother. A pause, and then she said, sounding a little touchy, "Okay, sure. Right...five minutes."

She returned the phone to her purse, and then sent Noah and me a smile I didn't believe for one second.

"My mother dropped me off here," she explained. "It's silly, but she thought it was better if she chauffeured me around town for now."

"Is she staying here until the trial, too?" I asked, trying not to sound too cheered by that prospect. After all, if her mother was lurking in the background, there was probably a lower chance of Shelby trying to get between Noah and me.

If that was even a prospect at all. Just because I didn't particularly like the woman didn't mean I should ascribe all sorts of nefarious motivations to her.

Shelby's mouth pursed slightly. "Yes, she's staying with me," she replied. "That's why we found a bigger house to rent for the summer. Luckily, she doesn't have to work, so she can be with me the whole time."

I recalled that Noah had mentioned how Shelby's father had passed away a while back. He must have had a heck of a life insurance policy, or maybe they were the kind of family who lived off their investments and trust funds.

Either way, that seemed to explain why Mrs. Howard had the ready cash to cover her daughter's bail. "That's nice," I said, knowing even as I spoke what a feeble response it was. Still, what else was I supposed to say? It definitely wasn't my place to ask questions about how Shelby's mother was in a position to drop everything to be at her daughter's side.

Shelby's phone pinged again, and she looked down at the screen.

"My mother's waiting outside," she announced. "So I need to get going. But thank you, Charity, for agreeing to help out."

She got up from the couch then, and Noah and I rose as well. "I think I have something I want to try," I told her, since a trickle of an idea had just begun to work its way through my brain. "I'll let you know if anything comes of it."

She looked as though she wanted to ask more questions, but her phone pinged again. Another text from her mother, I guessed, asking what was taking her so long.

"Sounds great," Shelby said, then hurried out the door.

Left alone, Noah and I looked at each other for a moment. Then he managed a very lopsided smile.

"Looks like I owe you some dinner."

* * *

We were able to get right in at Mercy Tavern, probably because it was the middle of the week and most of the vacationers had long since departed. Noah and I slid into a booth at the back, and after we'd ordered a bottle of wine, he sent me a frank look.

"Thanks for doing this. I know Shelby kind of put you on the spot."

I didn't bother to protest, since that was exactly what she'd done. Instead, I picked up my glass of ice water, took a sip, and replied, "It's all right. If I were in a similar situation, I'd like to think I'd get the same kind of help."

He didn't respond right away, but instead

tapped his fingers against his water glass, expression thoughtful. Was he pondering whether Shelby would have offered her assistance if our situations had been reversed?

Somehow, I had a feeling she wouldn't be quite so generous.

When Noah spoke, however, he didn't address what I'd just said, and instead asked, "So...what's your plan?"

I'd had the thought that I needed to go back to the scene of the crime and cast a scrying spell, and see if that might offer some much-needed clues. Getting into the cottage shouldn't be a problem; it was still an active crime scene, but sooner or later, the Salem P.D. would be done with it. Once Hannah had been given the all-clear, I could just ask her to let me in and poke around. Since she and my mother had been friends since grade school, I knew she wouldn't turn me down.

But because that plan included using magic, I knew I couldn't tell Noah anything about what I intended. Instead, I gave him a smile I hoped was mysterious rather than foolish, and said, "Oh, I don't want to jinx it."

Most men probably would have pressed me on the issue. Noah, I was learning, was cut from very different cloth, so he only responded, "Fair enough. And even if nothing comes of it, at least you tried."

"I'm glad you at least don't have unrealistic expectations," I remarked, and he smiled.

"Well, Shelby's always been one of those people who wants what she wants, and she doesn't tend to let reality get in the way. But I know you're not a private detective or anything. It just seems like you definitely got ahead of the police in the case of Milo's dognapper."

I shrugged, and was saved from having to reply by the arrival of the waitress with our bottle of merlot. Once it had been uncorked and she'd poured some wine into our glasses, she asked if we were ready to order.

Luckily, I knew the menu well enough that I was able to ask for baked mac and cheese, giving Noah enough time to take a quick glance at the bill of fare and order some steak tips for himself. With that taken care of, the waitress departed, leaving the two of us to gaze awkwardly across the table at one another.

"But we can worry about that later," he said. "Did you still want to bring your cat to the clinic tomorrow morning so I can take a look at her?"

I blinked. What with everything that had been going on, I'd almost forgotten about my plan to take Cinny over to Noah's clinic so he could examine her and see if there was any physical reason as to why she wouldn't be able to have a litter.

"Um, yes," I replied quickly. "If it's okay."

"It's fine," he said. "I've got some routine shots and exams scheduled, but no big surgeries, so I know I can squeeze her in. Does nine o'clock work?"

I assured him it did—that was actually perfect, because I could take care of the errand before I had to open the shop at ten—and we moved on to other topics, among them his friends Jared and Kathy wanting to know if we could come over on Saturday night for a barbecue. They'd probably extended the invitation before this whole mess with Shelby occurred, but it seemed clear that Noah wanted to go...and that they already considered the two of us a couple, even if nothing formal had been said.

It all felt wonderfully normal, and I found myself saying that sounded like fun, and then asked if they wanted me to bring anything. No, I wasn't a full-on kitchen witch like some of the other members of my coven, but I could still whip up a mean batch of German potato salad when the occasion arose.

Noah said he'd check, and the remainder of the meal was refreshingly uneventful.

Somehow, I doubted the rest of my week would be the same.

* * *

Cinny was amenable to going to the vet once I assured her that Noah was just going to take a look, and wasn't going to stick any needles in her.

"I hate shots," she told me, her tone emphatic.

"So do I," I replied with a smile. "But you've already had your vaccinations. This is just to see if there's any reason why you can't have a litter of kittens. Once we've got that figured out, we'll know better what to do next."

The cat seemed reassured by my comment, and went quietly into her carrier. Technically, since she was a familiar and therefore much more cooperative than your ordinary garden-variety cat, she probably could have ridden on the front seat, but I didn't want Noah to think I was being careless with an animal I was "fostering."

Milo—even though it was clear to me that he adored Noah—was perfectly happy to stay home alone if it meant not having to go with us to the vet's office.

"I don't like those places," he declared, and I bent down to give him a scratch behind the ears.

"Well, I'm not a fan of doctor's offices, so I get it," I told him. "We'll just have to promise to both stay healthy and far away from them."

The dog wagged his tail, and I went ahead and picked up the cat carrier and headed out the door. It was another blissfully beautiful early summer day, with a fresh breeze off the ocean and the sun just warm enough that it felt friendly and gentle, rather than blasting down on me. As I set Cinny's carrier on the front seat of my Land Rover, I found myself reflecting that this would be a perfect day to play hooky, to run off with Noah and have a picnic on the beach or something.

But we both had to work, so that wasn't going to happen. Also, I needed to call Hannah Owens—she hated text messages—and find out when she thought I'd be able to head over to the cottage and see if I could pick up on anything about the crime that had happened there the night before. I wouldn't be able to go over until the Salem P.D. cleared the scene, but I was hoping that event might coincide with my shop closing at five o'clock.

Well, I'd wait until I was done at Noah's clinic. It was too early to call unless it was an emergency, anyway.

The parking lot at the clinic wasn't too full when I pulled in, telling me his assertion that he didn't have a busy schedule that morning had been correct. No reason to think otherwise, of course, but still, it was nice to know he hadn't been down-playing the busyness of his schedule just so I wouldn't feel bad about coming in.

In fact, he was there to greet me when I entered the waiting room, Cinny's cat carrier hanging from one hand. He didn't give me a hug —probably because his office assistant was sitting at the front desk and giving us a curious glance from behind her glasses—but his smile was bright as the sunny day outside as he took the carrier from me.

"Come on back," he said, guiding me past his assistant's desk and down a corridor with rows of doors on either side. I could hear dogs barking near the end of the hallway, and guessed that was where the animals who had to stay overnight for observation were boarded.

However, we went through a door long before we got to the end of the hall, a typical exam room with a table in the center and various posters about vaccinations and animal diseases posted on the wall. After Noah set the cat carrier down on the exam table, he sent me a quizzical glance.

"Will she be okay with me taking her out of the carrier, or do you think you should do it?"

"She'll be fine," I assured him. "She's a very mellow cat."

He nodded, then unlatched the front of the carrier. At once, Cinny emerged, looking singularly unperturbed by her surroundings.

Because we weren't alone, she didn't try to speak, but she did send me a questioning look. I tilted my head ever so slightly, and she sat down and licked a paw, clearly waiting for Noah to do whatever he needed to do.

Still smiling, he commented, "You're right—

she is pretty mellow. I can see why she and Milo get along so well."

"Yes, they've definitely turned out to be fast friends," I agreed. "But friends or not, she's supposed to go back to her owner at the end of the week."

Which made me a little sad. I liked Cinny a lot, and it was fun to see her and Milo hanging out together. However, I reminded myself that I couldn't keep every animal I worked with, or my house would soon be overrun by wayward familiars. Milo's had been a special case, but Doris was waiting to get Cinnamon back, no matter what happened this week.

Noah set the cat carrier on the floor, then got out a light and checked the cat's eyes and ears and mouth, and ran a hand over her tummy. "She's strong and healthy, probably around four or five years old," he said. "Did her owner ever say why she didn't have her spayed?"

I gave what I hoped was a convincing shrug. "Not really, but it sounds like she's exclusively an indoor cat, so maybe Doris didn't think it was necessary."

That response earned me a slight frown. "Maybe there wasn't any risk of the cat getting pregnant, but it's still annoying to have to deal with one going into heat a couple of times a year."

In general, I had to agree with his observation.

However, since familiars didn't have offspring and therefore didn't go into heat, it really wasn't an issue in this particular case.

Obviously, I couldn't tell Noah that.

I settled for lifting my shoulders again and said, "I honestly don't know why Cinny's owner wasn't worried about it."

For a second or two, I thought Noah might decide to press the matter further. However, I allowed myself an inner sigh of relief when he responded, "Well, I suppose that's her business. I'm going to perform the gynecological exam now to see what we're dealing with."

"Thanks for the warning," I said. "I think I'll just go look at one of those posters over there while you work."

And I gestured toward a poster warning about the dangers of not having your pet's teeth cleaned regularly.

Noah chuckled. "Probably a good idea."

A quick glance at Cinny told me she looked more resigned than anything else, as if she knew she'd signed up for this and just had to grit her teeth until Noah was done with the exam. Satisfied that she was going to keep calm, I went over to the poster and got way more up close and personal with images of canine receding gums than I'd ever wanted to. Still, it was much better than standing by and watching the cat get probed.

An uncomfortable couple of minutes passed, and then Noah said, "That's strange."

"What's the matter?" I asked, even as a shiver of worry passed through me. What if there really was something wrong with Cinnamon?

"Nothing," he said quickly. "But I thought you said she hadn't been spayed."

"She wasn't," I replied. After all, there was no reason to spay a cat who never went into heat and would never have kittens.

He laid a gentle hand on the cat's head. Whatever he'd done, it appeared to be over with now, and Cinny sat calmly, waiting for the vet's verdict.

Noah, on the other hand, didn't look quite so calm. Not upset, exactly, just...perplexed, brows drawn together and mouth pursed slightly.

"She doesn't have any ovaries," he told me. "When a cat is spayed, sometimes just the ovaries are removed, and sometimes a vet will take out both the ovaries and the uterus. In Cinny's case, it doesn't look as though she ever had her ovaries to begin with. I can't see any signs of scar tissue, nothing that would show she's had a previous surgery. It's almost as if she was never born with them at all."

Interesting. I wondered if that was a side effect of becoming a familiar, or whether all familiars had some kind of similar birth defect that made them perfect candidates to be a witch's companion.

There was quite possibly some subtle magic going on here, something I'd certainly never heard about before.

I'd definitely have to ask Grace Bowersby about it when I had the chance.

For now, though, I needed to focus on the practical. Whatever the reason for Cinny's utterly sterile biology, Noah had definitely zeroed in on the reason why she'd never had any kittens...or ever would.

Judging by the frown the cat currently wore, it appeared obvious enough to me that she understood what Noah was saying, and didn't like it a single bit. Fortunately, though, it seemed as if she'd also realized she needed to stay quiet until the two of us were well away from the vet clinic.

"Does that happen very often?" I asked, hoping my hesitation hadn't been too obvious.

Noah shook his head. "I've never seen it before. But sometimes organs just fail to develop—that's something called 'agenesis.' In Cinny's case, they weren't organs she needed to live a happy, healthy life, so her condition wouldn't have been discovered before now."

"Well, it answers a few questions," I said. "It's too bad, though—there aren't many female ginger cats to begin with, so it would have been nice for Cinny to pass on that trait."

Once again, he ran a gentle hand over Cinnamon's back. She arched, leaning into the caress, a gesture that told me, while she might have been upset by the news she'd just received, she definitely didn't blame Noah for her condition.

"Anyway," I went on, "thanks for taking a look. I won't take up any more of your time—I know you probably have other patients to check on."

For a second, Noah's eyes met mine, and held. Although a veterinarian's examination room was probably one of the least romantic places on the planet, I couldn't quite hold back the delicious little shiver that went down my back as our gazes locked.

Damn, that man was gorgeous. The white lab coat was just icing on the cake.

"You know I don't mind making time for you," he said softly.

And I would have been more than happy to make all the time in the world for him. But I had a store that needed opening, and I kind of doubted anyone in the waiting room with a dog that needed its rabies shots updated would be too thrilled with either of us for wasting their time.

I smiled. "Good to know," I said, my tone purposely light. "I've got to get to work, though. But maybe you can come over tonight and we can get takeout or something?"

As soon as the words left my mouth, his gaze flicked away from mine. "I wish I could," he said.

"Shelby's mom really wants to meet with me after work, though. She wants to hear from me about what we saw in the cottage, so I said I'd talk to her."

If she was really all that interested in fact-finding, you'd think she'd want to talk to me as well. I wouldn't push it, though. For all I knew, it was a sore subject with Mrs. Howard that Noah had started seeing someone new, even though he and her daughter had broken up a year earlier and she'd obviously moved on.

"Oh, that's fine," I said, praying I sounded casual. "I hope you can give them some information that will help Shelby's case."

"Me too," Noah responded at once. "Rain check? Let's do something Friday night."

"It's a date."

He came over and kissed me on the cheek, then helped me get Cinny in her cat carrier and even walked me all the way to the lobby door. A wave, and then I headed over to the place where my Land Rover was parked.

Was I disappointed that we wouldn't be able to see each other after work? Of course. At the same time, though, I realized I would be free tonight.

And I knew exactly what I needed to do with that time.

Chapter 6

Hindsight

Ginny moped all the way home, and I really couldn't blame her. Years ago, I'd decided I didn't want to have children, that I didn't want to run the risk of giving birth to a child, only to learn years later that she didn't have any magic and would have to be raised away from me and the world of witchcraft, but I could still empathize with the feelings the cat familiar must be experiencing, of longing for kittens and realizing that now she would never be able to have any.

Of course, in my particular case, I was starting to wonder if maybe I'd been too hasty in making my own decision not to have a family. Part of it had been born out of frustration with the utter wasteland that had been my love life, but now that I'd met Noah....

I wanted to push that thought right out of my

head. For one thing, we might have known each other casually for months, but we'd only been romantic for around a week, which wasn't exactly enough time to be making life-changing decisions based on what was still an extremely new relationship.

All the same, I'd never met anyone like him before. Not even close.

I took Cinny home and gave her a couple of extra salmon treats. No, that wasn't really adequate compensation for realizing she wouldn't be able to have the family she wanted, but I hoped she'd see I was doing my best to make her feel a little bit better.

She took the treats and ate them solemnly, then went and curled up next to Milo, who was lying on the rug in front of the fireplace. He seemed to sense she needed comforting, because he solemnly licked her on the ear and then sent me a quiet little look, one that seemed to signal he was going to make sure he took extra care of her today.

I flashed him a grateful smile, then told them both I'd be home this evening and would be sure to order something that would make them both happy.

After that, though, I needed to get going. As it was, I'd have to hit all the traffic lights just right in order to make it to the shop on time.

Which I did, unlocking the back door at

exactly 9:58. Sage was already there, so there really wasn't any reason for me to have worried, but still, I didn't want to look like a complete slacker.

"Busy morning?" she asked, an impish light in her hazel eyes. We both knew that I tried to get to the shop no later than a quarter 'til, just so I'd have plenty of time to make sure everything was tidy and the cash register stocked with bills and change for any shoppers who preferred to use the real stuff.

"Oh, I had to take Cinnamon to Noah to get looked at," I told her.

At once, Sage's expression sobered. "Is she okay?"

"She's fine," I replied. "I just needed to have him check on something."

I left it there, because, as much as I liked Sage, I wasn't going to share my charge's medical condition with her. No, that was between me and Cinny and Noah—and Doris eventually, I supposed, if Cinnamon decided she wanted to tell her mistress why she didn't need to worry about any kittens invading her space.

That was between the two of them, though; I wouldn't say anything to Doris unless Cinny gave me her express permission, and since the cat would be with me at least for the next couple of days, I figured we had time to work all that out.

In the meantime, I had to focus on getting the shop opened.

* * *

It was busy enough that I didn't have a chance to slip into the back and make a quick call to Hannah Owens until almost one o'clock. Luckily, she picked up on the second ring.

"Charity," she said, sounding surprised.

Maybe she hadn't heard that Noah and I had gone to the cottage to see Shelby, or maybe it was simply that she hadn't thought there would be any reason for me to reach out to her.

"Hi, Hannah," I replied. "Are the police still working on the crime scene at the cottage?"

A short, startled pause. "No," she said, her tone now turning cautious. "They finished up about an hour ago. I still need to have a cleaning crew come in, though. Why?"

"Can you wait on the cleaning crew?" I asked. "It's just that I want to go in and do some scrying, see if I can figure out anything about what happened there last night."

I couldn't see Hannah's face, but I still got the impression that her expression had shifted to one of amusement. "Are you going to be a full-time detective now, Charity?"

"Hardly," I assured her. "But Shelby asked me to help, and—"

"The young woman they arrested for killing her fiancé in *my* cottage?"

On the surface, I had to admit it all sounded pretty bad. "She didn't do it, Hannah," I said. "Honestly, she shouldn't have been arrested at all, but I have a feeling the police wanted to show they were doing something, considering there aren't any other viable suspects at the moment. I told Shelby I'd try to help, but the first thing I need to do is see if I can tap into the lingering energies in the place, and maybe get a better idea of what really happened. She was pretty shaken up when she tried to explain it to me and Noah, so it's possible she got some details wrong."

A heavy pause. I wondered if I needed to explain who Noah was, then realized that probably wasn't necessary. It wasn't as though I went around talking about my love life, but I didn't have to. My mother would have already spread the news about me dating one of the local vets to all the witches in the greater Salem area. Her gossiping could be annoying, but on the other hand, it helped cut down on lengthy explanations.

"All right," Hannah said. "If that young woman really is innocent, then of course you should do whatever you can to clear her name." A pause, and she added, "I assume I don't need to leave a key under the mat?"

"No," I said cheerfully, relieved I wouldn't have to go into any further detail as to exactly why I was helping Shelby Howard. "I can get in without one. And I'll lock up when I'm done."

"I know you will. Good luck with everything."

That was how we ended the call, which was fine. The important thing was that Hannah had given me her blessing, and that meant after work, I'd be able to get down to some *real* work.

* * *

It was still blazingly bright when I pulled up to Hannah's cottage; at that time of year, it wouldn't be full dark until almost nine. All the same, I couldn't quite hold back the little shiver that moved down my spine as I laid a hand on the door-knob and whispered the simple spell I'd been using to unlock doors since I was ten years old.

Open, unlock
So in I can walk

An audible *click* as the mechanism loosened, and then the door opened about an inch.

Even though I really didn't want to go inside, I made myself put my hand on the knob and push inside. Everything there was dark; it looked as though the forensics team had pulled down all the shades and hadn't left any lights on.

I fumbled for the switch and flicked it, and at

once the bulbs in the ceiling fan overhead turned on. For some reason, I'd expected to see a mess left behind by the investigators, but the room looked fairly tidy. Whoever had been managing the crime scene, it seemed they'd done their best to make it look as though nothing out of the ordinary had happened here.

Unfortunately, the obvious dark stain in the center of the flowered rug that covered most of the wooden floor ruined that impression.

I swallowed, and gave the blood spot a wide berth as I moved around the space. To be honest, I wasn't exactly sure what I was doing, because it wasn't as though I was a medium or someone who communicated with the spirits. No, I was just a witch with a decent knack for making potions and tinctures, and a unique talent for talking to other witches' familiars.

Anyway, I didn't sense anything out of the ordinary, except maybe an odd sort of metallic tang on the air, possibly something left behind from the chemicals the forensics people had used to conduct their investigation of the site. I certainly didn't hear any ghostly voices speaking to me from beyond, no cold spots or icy hands on the back of my neck.

And thank God for that.

The cottage wasn't very big, maybe around eight or nine hundred square feet, with one bedroom, one bathroom, and a dinky little kitchen.

Because it was so small, the main living area was mostly open, with a sitting area to one side and a dining area on the other. The kitchen occupied the space toward the back of the house, down a short hallway, an area that was echoed on the other side of the hall by the home's single bedroom and bathroom.

I'd made a quick detour to my house so I could get my silver scrying bowl, and I set it on the round table in the dining area, then filled it from the plastic jug of distilled water I'd brought with me. Moon water generally worked best for these sorts of enchantments, but I'd already used up my current supply while trying to find Darla Fitzgerald's killer and wouldn't be able to replenish those stores for a couple more weeks, when the moon would be full again.

Anyway, distilled water worked in a pinch, since it was pure if not technically enchanted.

Once the bowl was filled, I sat down at one of the table's three small chairs and placed my hands against its silver sides, closing my eyes so I could focus on the water I'd just poured and the answer I was seeking.

Help me now, oh liquid clear
Let your waters tell the tale
Of what happened here
So the guilty go to jail!

A pedestrian rhyme, sure, but spells didn't care if you were Shakespeare or not—they just needed a focus for the magic, a place for it to concentrate.

The distilled water inside the bowl shivered and then went quiet. I held myself still as well, knowing I needed to let the magic work its way into the liquid and, with any luck, show me exactly what had happened in the cottage the night before.

Another small tremor of the water's surface, as though an unseen wind had moved over it, and then it became smooth and flat again.

Now it was utterly reflective, only it seemed to be showing me the night before, and not the cottage's living space as it was now. The ceiling fan was on, making the little valances over the windows flutter ever so slightly, and it was fully lit, along with the lamp on the three-legged table that flanked one side of the sofa.

Shelby and a man I guessed must be Trevor Miller were sitting on that couch, talking heatedly. The mirror didn't transmit sound, unfortunately, but their expressions and their agitated hand gestures seemed to indicate they weren't exactly having a pleasant chat.

Was it possible that Shelby really had killed Trevor in a fit of anger? She didn't seem physically capable of such a thing, but....

Whatever the argument was about, it seemed to be ending, because Shelby got up from the sofa and walked over to the window, and Trevor followed a second or two later. He was tall, with blond hair just this side of sandy, and the sort of even, all-American features that probably would have looked perfect in college pictures of his rowing club, or whatever else he'd done on the side besides fencing. Definitely attractive, although not as good-looking as Noah.

All right, I was probably a little biased on that particular subject.

The two of them exchanged a few more words, and he put a hand on her arm. She smiled up at him, looking hesitant, and then he bent down and kissed her.

It felt oddly intrusive to watch that embrace, even though I knew I was only seeing what had taken place here in the cottage the day before. No one could have accused me of being a voyeur, but....

To my relief, the kiss didn't last very long. Trevor appeared to chuckle and said something to Shelby, and she leaned her head toward her purse—an oversized Louis Vuitton tote that I knew must have cost a chunk of change—where it sat on the small round table off to one side. He went to fetch the bag, she looped it over her arm, and the two of them went out. I couldn't tell whether she really had forgotten to lock the door, since the scrying mirror only showed what had happened in the room where I now stood, and not anything that might be taking place on the other side of the front door.

The water in the scrying bowl darkened, and for a second or two, I was worried that the enchantment had already petered out and I'd have to start all over again. To my relief, though, another of those small ripples moved across the surface of the liquid, and the scene of the cottage's living room reappeared.

It seemed as if some time had passed, because Shelby was now putting her purse back on the side table, and the two of them looked much more cheerful. She said something to Trevor and he must have replied in the affirmative, because she sent him an answering smile and headed down the hallway into the kitchen.

As I watched, I stiffened. Unless I wasn't recalling her story correctly, this was the moment when the intruder entered the cottage and attacked Trevor.

Sure enough, almost as soon as she'd disappeared down the short hall that separated the main living area from the kitchen, a dark figure emerged from the bedroom.

Yes, that was definitely the "ninja" from Shelby's account of what had happened. The person looked as though he—or she—was around Trevor's height, so maybe six feet tall or so.

However, their height was the only thing that was equally matched. The ninja came at Trevor in a dark blur, and the two of them wrestled for a moment before Trevor was knocked off balance, arms flailing as he tried to remain upright. A flash of steel as the black-clad intruder pulled a sword from a black leather scabbard at his side, and then the blade was thrust in Trevor's back. He fell to the floor face down, in exactly the same place where Noah and I had seen him when we ran over to the cottage in response to Shelby's panicked phone call.

Even though the moving images in the bowl were utterly silent, I still couldn't help wincing. Watching this was completely different from the impersonal experience of viewing a movie or television show. These were real people, and although I'd never met Trevor, witnessing his death like this might as well have been a punch to my stomach.

I wouldn't look away, however. If there was even the slightest clue in this magical playback that might allow me to figure out who had killed Trevor Miller, then I needed to keep watching, no matter what.

The ninja stood over Trevor's body for a moment, his—or her, although I was doubting more and more that the killer had been a woman—tall, lean form utterly still. Then his head lifted as Shelby came barreling into the room, obviously responding to the sounds of their scuffle.

Was that the slightest bit of hesitation? Possibly, but since I couldn't rewind the images in the mirror, I could only keep watching as her mouth opened in the wide "O" of a scream, and the ninja seemed to recover from his paralysis and ran toward her, pushing her out of the way as he headed toward the kitchen and, I assumed, the rear entrance to the cottage.

Just as she'd described, she stumbled against the wall and stood there for a moment, breathing heavily, hair falling forward so I couldn't see her expression. Then, with halting steps, she headed toward the living room, where the body of her dead fiancé lay prone on the incongruously flowered carpet.

The image faded then, and I somehow knew it wouldn't be coming back unless I cast another spell...and maybe not even then. This kind of magic was often tricky, and I'd be the first to admit I wasn't an expert at it, even though I utilized it from time to time when I knew no other magical intervention would give me the information I needed.

I straightened up and glanced behind me, at that telltale stain in the rug. Would it ever come out, or would Hannah have to replace it?

Honestly, I didn't think keeping such a relic in a place where she expected to have vacationers stay was a very good idea. Maybe Trevor's ghost wasn't lingering here...at least, I hadn't seen any indication that his spirit had decided to stay and haunt the little cottage...but still, it was probably best to get rid of as many pieces of evidence as possible. It seemed a little strange to me that the detectives investigating the murder hadn't hauled the rug off to be analyzed in a lab, although I'd be the first to admit I really didn't know how such things worked. I supposed they might have already gotten all the evidence they needed from it and didn't see the point in taking the bulky carpet with them.

As far as I could tell from what I'd seen in the mirror, everything else seemed to have happened pretty much exactly the way she'd said it had. I wondered if I would have been able to recount those events with as much clarity if our situations had been reversed.

I didn't want to think about that...mostly because, if I'd been in Shelby's shoes, that would have been Noah's body lying on the flowered rug in the living room, not that of Trevor Miller.

Just thinking of Noah made me wish I could talk to him about what I'd seen in the mirror. Unfortunately, that was about the last thing I'd ever be able to do. Things were still far too new between us for me to ever let him know there was a lot more to me than met the eye.

No, for now I'd have to hold this information close...and maybe at some point try to decide what I was going to do about it.

Chapter 7

Mama Don't Preach

Howevever, I wasn't so troubled about what I'd seen in the scrying mirror that I didn't take a short detour on my way home so I could pick up some tacos from Spitfire, along with an extra little container of their carne asada. I thought that would be a special treat for both Milo and Cinny, since the cat seemed to be okay with people food every once in a while if it was something especially tempting.

As I pulled into the driveway, though, I couldn't help wondering about Noah's interview with Shelby's mom. Were mother and daughter over at his house even now?

Maybe. He hadn't really said exactly what time they planned to meet, only that he wouldn't be available this evening. It still rankled a little that they hadn't wanted to get my input as well, but I supposed it was possible they thought I'd only repeat what Noah was going to tell them.

Either way, I was on my own this evening, and I knew I needed to deal with it.

All right, not entirely on my own. Milo and Cinny met me at the back door, obviously happy to see the bag of takeout in my hand.

"Yes, there's some for you," I assured them as I headed over to the counter so I could set down both the food and my purse. Usually, I'd leave it on the kitchen table, but this seemed much easier.

However, Milo wasn't so preoccupied with the food that he didn't ask, "No Noah tonight?"

"No," I replied, hoping my tone wasn't too curt. "He had something else he needed to do. But we'll be seeing each other tomorrow night."

"That's good," the dog said, and I felt my mouth quirk. If I'd known my adopted familiar was going to be just as much of a noodge on the topic of my dating life as my mother, I might not have been quite so quick to let him stay with me.

No, that wasn't true. I loved Milo, and he obviously liked seeing Noah and me together. Since we were definitely on the same page when it came to my relationship with Noah Jenkins, I'd be a hypocrite if I gave my animal companion too much grief over his matchmaking.

"For now, though," I said, "it's the three of us and tacos. Who wants some carne asada?"

Of course, both Milo and Cinny said they did, although I was careful not to give either of them too much. Still, it was enough that they looked enormously satisfied when we congregated in front of the TV following the meal, and I chose something fun and lighthearted to watch, something that would distract me and the animals, and keep all our minds off the murder that had happened less than a mile from the spot where we sat in my living room.

I had a feeling I succeeded more with the animals than I did myself.

* * *

No text from Noah that night, either; I checked before I started getting ready for bed. I tried to tell myself I had no idea how late Mrs. Howard might have stayed at his place, and besides, some of what they had said might have been strictly between the three of them. Yes, Noah and I had been spending a lot of time together lately, and it seemed to me he was being as serious about our relationship progressing as I was...maybe even more so...but it wasn't as though we were joined at the hip.

Not even close.

After I lay down, though, I couldn't stop myself from dwelling on that brief image I'd seen in the scrying mirror, how the ninja intruder had knocked Shelby out of the way as he fled rather than pushing her to the floor. She'd looked startled but not necessarily in pain.

Which didn't mean all that much. Although I had no idea who the murderer was or why he would have gone after Trevor, this seemed like a personal crime to me. If that was the case—if the intruder had gone to the cottage specifically to kill Trevor Miller—then obviously, he wouldn't have wanted to waste time wrestling with Shelby. No, he would have just wanted to get her out of the way so he could be as far from the scene as possible before the police showed up. Because he was masked, it wasn't as though he had to worry about her identifying him in a lineup or anything.

I closed my eyes and told myself that lying awake all night and fretting about the situation wasn't going to change anything. Yes, it felt awful not being able to tell Noah about what I'd seen in the scrying mirror, but as much as I wanted to help him out here...I wasn't going to lie to myself and say this was all for Shelby's sake...I absolutely could not betray the witch community.

Well, all wasn't lost. I'd see Sage at work tomorrow, and maybe she could help me pick up on something I'd overlooked. I didn't see a problem discussing the case with my assistant, since I knew she would keep quiet if I asked her, and probably would be glad that I trusted her enough to take her into my confidence.

And with that plan in mind, I was finally able to fall asleep.

* * *

Sage and I couldn't talk right away, unfortunately, because a big tour bus had disgorged its passengers in front of my store at five minutes before ten, and as soon as I unlocked the front door to Full Moon Apothecary, we were bombarded.

I told myself it was okay, that I should be happy to have the business. Even so, I couldn't help letting out a small sigh of relief once the group of elderly tourists were finished inspecting my wares and had moved on to Witch City Wicks, the candle shop next door.

"Whew," Sage said once we were safely alone. "I wonder if it's going to be like this all summer."

True, business had been brisker than usual lately, but that could have simply been a fluke. "I guess we'll just have to wait and see," I said.

Sage nodded, but then she tilted her head slightly, something in the narrowing of her hazel eyes telling me she'd noticed I seemed preoccupied.

"It's kind of crazy, this thing with Noah's ex," she said.

I hadn't even looked at the paper this morning...I still got it delivered, more to support another local business rather than because I actually had time to read the thing...but I supposed I shouldn't be too surprised that the news of the murder had reached the Salem *Herald*. And since I knew I was feeling a little off that morning, I guessed it was inevitable that Sage would have picked up on the reason for my malaise.

"It is," I said, then paused. "I've been doing a little poking around on my own, but obviously, I can't tell Noah exactly what I've been up to."

My assistant nodded, a spark of interest lighting up her green-brown eyes. "Want to talk about it?"

Of course I did.

So I related what I'd seen in the scrying mirror, explaining how the murderer had shoved Shelby out of the way rather than attempting to make her his second victim.

"I know it's probably not a big deal," I concluded. "But still...something feels a little off about what happened."

"The killer was probably just targeting Shelby's fiancé," Sage said, echoing my own thoughts of the day before. "I mean, once the deed was done, he'd want to get the hell out of there, right?"

"Makes sense," I said, then figured it was probably better to abandon the topic until I had more information to work with...or a flash of inspiration, which didn't seem very likely at the moment. "So, what did the paper say about the murder?"

"Not a whole lot," Sage replied. She paused for a moment as a young family with the father pushing a stroller passed by the store's front window, but since they kept going, she apparently guessed it was okay to proceed. "I mean, they said that Shelby Howard's fiancé was found murdered in the cottage Hannah owns, but they didn't give any details, only said it was an 'ongoing investigation.'" Another pause, except I knew by the speculative gleam in my assistant's eyes that she'd only stopped in order to figure out the best way to ask me the next question. "Do *you* know what happened?"

"I do," I said calmly.

"Well, spill it!"

Since I'd already basically sworn her to secrecy, I didn't see the problem in telling her the truth. "Someone dressed all in black broke in and stuck a sword in the man's back."

Sage stared at me, wide-eyed. "Seriously?"

"Seriously," I echoed. "I guess the sword belonged to Trevor, Shelby's fiancé. I don't have any idea how the killer got it, though, since it sounds as if the sword was kept in his office, and I kind of doubted he would have driven all the way to Salem to see her without making sure his office was locked up and secure before he left."

"Seems like a weird way to kill someone," Sage observed, and I shrugged.

"I thought so, too. But I guess one thing you can say about a sword is that it's quiet. It's not like using a gun and having to worry about having a silencer, or whatever."

She nodded, expression pensive. Like me, she was probably wondering what could have happened to cause someone to hold such a horrible grudge against another human being, and to use that grudge as motivation to commit such a terrible crime.

Practical reasons for using a sword versus a gun aside, it was an extremely personal kind of murder. You couldn't stand yards away from your victim if you were using a sword.

No, you had to get close, had to feel the blade sink into someone's flesh.

I couldn't quite hold back the shudder which went through me at that mental image, and Sage nodded, as if she'd been harboring the same thoughts.

"It's kind of gruesome," she agreed. "And I'm also really hoping that this murder was personal. I don't like the idea of some kind of ninja guy dressed in black running around Salem with swords."

Neither did I. However, before I'd left the cottage, I'd cast a quick "detect peril" spell and hadn't gotten any kind of response, telling me that my hometown was currently safe from any further sword-wielding assailants. Before I could reassure Sage on that subject, though, the bell on the shop door jingled faintly as a man and woman came in to the apothecary.

I could tell right away the newcomers weren't our usual kind of customer, not like the locals who subscribed to alternate forms of medicine or the tourists who dropped in and picked up a few odds and ends out of curiosity more than anything else.

The woman looked as though she was probably in her late fifties, although she might have been older, her taut jaw line and nearly wrinkle-free skin the result of extremely subtle and skilled surgical intervention. Her white linen shirt was similarly free of wrinkles, and although she wore jeans, they were so crisp and dark that I wouldn't have been surprised to learn she had them dry-cleaned to preserve that off-the-rack freshness. And the man with her was equally distinguished, maybe a few years older, with the kind of silvery hair that told me it had probably been blond when he was younger.

"Are you Charity Hughes?" the woman asked after a quick assessing glance that took in both me and my assistant, and obviously concluded that Sage was too young to be the shop owner. The man with her—her husband?—seemed satisfied to let his companion do the talking, although his sharp gray eyes looked as though they didn't miss very much.

"I am," I said politely. I got the feeling the woman wasn't here to buy anything, but it never hurt to be professional, especially with someone who wore rocks like the ones that glinted on her ears and her left hand. No, they weren't flashy, but the studs that shone from behind her expertly tinted blonde hair and the double bands on her ring finger had probably cost more than the entire contents of my house. The man only wore a wedding band, but I guessed the white metal was platinum, not white gold.

"Good," the woman said, and paused, sending a weighted look in Sage's direction.

My assistant, who usually wasn't cowed by anyone, blurted out, "I need to check the stockroom," and hurried off toward the back of the shop, leaving the two strangers and me alone.

Well, until the next customer came in.

"I am Lorna Miller," the woman said, giving the words the same kind of weight as if her last name had been Rockefeller or Vanderbilt. Maybe it had been before she was married. "And this is my husband, Thad Miller. Trevor was our son."

Uh-oh. I had no idea how the Millers had gotten my name or learned where the store was located, but I guessed that Shelby must have said something and they had done the rest of the legwork to find me. "I'm so sorry for your loss," I murmured.

Lorna Miller's chin lifted. The skin beneath it was as taut as mine, telling me that she must have gotten some expert work done there. "We didn't *lose* our son," she said sharply, while her husband gave a single stiff nod, as if to indicate his agreement with her remark. "He was taken from us. And the police have been absolutely no help, not even that nice Detective Falco."

I had no idea who Detective Falco was, since all witches did their best to avoid any kind of contact with the police. And considering how Sage had just told me a few minutes earlier that the police currently didn't have any leads, I couldn't really argue with Lorna Miller's assessment of the situation. "Well, they've just started the investigation," I replied, hoping my comment sounded diplomatic enough.

She sniffed, while her husband crossed his arms. "I do not have high expectations. However, Shelby Howard said something about how you recently solved a murder all on your own."

Well, at least I didn't have to speculate any more about how Lorna Miller and her husband had tracked me down. "That was more blind luck than anything else," I said. "I'm certainly not a private detective or anything. In fact," I added as a thought occurred to me, "I had help from a P.I. when I was trying to figure out who'd kidnapped my dog. I can give you her contact information, if you want. She's the wife of one of Noah Jenkins' vet school friends."

At my mention of Noah, Lorna's expertly plumped lips thinned a bit, and Thad Miller's gray brows drew together. Most likely, neither one of them liked being reminded that Shelby had been engaged to someone else before she met Trevor.

"If we'd wanted a private detective, we would have hired one," Lorna said, her tone as taut as her jaw. "In this particular case, Thad and I both think it's much better to work with someone local, someone who knows Salem."

That description definitely fit me well enough. You couldn't get much more local than me. On the other hand....

"You think the murderer is someone local?" I inquired.

"Yes, we do," Thad responded, speaking for the first time. His gray eyes reminded me of mist, shrouded, unreadable. "Our son was perfectly fine until he came to this damn town."

I bristled at that description of my home-town...and then reminded myself that Thad Miller had just suffered a devastating loss and probably wasn't paying much attention to what he said or how he said it.

On the other hand, I got the uneasy impression that neither Thad nor his wife were the type of people to care much about how their words affected those they considered beneath them. And even though I thought I was doing just fine for myself, owning my own store and house before the time I was thirty still didn't put me in the kind of economic bracket that allowed me to walk around with probably a hundred thousand dollars' worth of jewelry on my person and not bat an eye.

"Possibly," I allowed, and reminded myself I didn't want to get in an argument with a man whose son had been murdered the day before yesterday. "But do you know whether he had any enemies, anyone who might have held a grudge against him for some reason?"

At that question, which I'd asked innocently enough, Lorna drew herself up, blue eyes snapping fire, even as Thad's storm-colored brows turned thunderous again.

"Absolutely not," Lorna declared. "Everyone loved Trevor. He had many, many friends, quite a few of whom were people he'd remained close to even after graduating from Yale."

I knew it was a touchy question, but I told myself I needed to ask it anyway. If nothing else, it might tell me a little bit more about Trevor, who was still not much more than a cipher to me. "What about at his work?"

If possible, Thad Miller looked even more offended than he had a moment earlier. "He was a mainstay of my architectural firm...and my employees are *very* loyal," he told me, his tone telling me he would brook no arguments on that particular topic. "The business has been in my family for four generations. I have the grandsons of architects who worked there back in the forties and fifties coming to work for me. There is absolutely no one at Miller & Miller who isn't absolutely loyal to my family, and to Trevor."

Well, that was a nice story. I'd been my own boss for years, but I still remembered working at a couple of local businesses back when I was in high school and college. Some of those experiences had been good...and others definitely not so good. What they all had in common, though, was the unwavering belief on the part of those companies' owners that they were great places to work and that the people in charge treated their employees fairly, whether or not that assessment was at all accurate.

Which was why I doubted Thad really knew what the situation was like on the ground at Miller & Miller, so to speak, despite being the boss. However, I wouldn't challenge his suppositions, partly because I didn't want to get into an argument, and partly because I thought doing so would be extraordinarily rude, considering the loss he and his wife had just suffered.

On the other hand, there was nothing stopping me from poking around a bit.

As soon as that thought passed through my mind, I wanted to shake my head at myself. A minute earlier, I'd been advising the Millers to hire a private detective, and now I was thinking about conducting interviews at their family's architectural firm?

"Well, that's nice to hear," I said neutrally. "And since it sounds as though Trevor was universally well-liked, I'm not sure what you expect me to do."

Lorna sent me a disbelieving look, even as Thad's overworked eyebrows lifted slightly. "You know people here, don't you?" she challenged me. "People come into your shop and chat, don't they? I don't see how it would be too difficult to pay attention and see if anything raises a red flag for you."

Was it worth pointing out that most killers didn't exactly drop into the local apothecary shop and trade tips on the best way to bury a blade in someone's back?

Probably not.

"I know a lot of people," I said, doing my best to sound casual, matter-of-fact. "But Salem's a big city. We've got almost 45,000 people here. It's not as if I could possibly know all of them, or what they're up to."

Another of those narrow-eyed glances, this one of withering scorn. "Well, of course not," Lorna replied, while Thad gave a slight nod of agreement. "At the same time, you're in a position to hear more than we would...not that we plan on staying here for any length of time. We're only here now because we're waiting for the medical examiner to release Trevor to us."

Ouch. I hadn't thought about that, but it made sense that the coroner's office wouldn't need to hang on to Trevor's body for very long. After all, it was pretty obvious that he'd died of internal trauma, which was generally what happened when you got a two-foot-long blade stuck inside you.

Even though I had no idea how much help I could be, I murmured, "I'll see what I can do. May I have one of your phone numbers in case I come up with any leads?"

Lorna's expression relaxed a bit, and I could tell she was glad I hadn't continued to protest, that I'd apparently given in to her demand couched as a request. While her husband looked on, she reached in her purse, got out a heavy silver card case, and then removed a piece of buff-colored parchment printed with her name and phone number.

"You can leave a message here," she said as she handed me the card, words that seemed to indicate maybe the number wasn't her personal cell, but simply a place where people could record a voicemail. I couldn't help noticing that Thad hadn't offered his own contact information, but possibly they'd already decided that Lorna should handle the bulk of the back-and-forth while he went back to work.

Actually, that was fine by me. I still doubted I'd be able to unearth anything useful, but in case I did, it seemed a lot easier to leave Lorna a message rather than have to hold another conversation with her...or her intimidating husband.

"Thanks," I said, and slipped the card into a pocket in my dress.

Lorna apparently decided she'd accomplished what she and Thad had come here for, because she responded, "Obviously, we expect you to understand that this conversation was confidential. But get in touch if you hear anything," before gliding out of the shop in her Cole Haan sandals, her husband following a foot or so behind her.

A moment later, Sage stuck her head out of the stockroom, "Is the coast clear?"

"It is," I replied.

Her face was full of questions, but she didn't get the chance to ask them, because a group of older people, obviously tourists, came into the shop right then and began peppering me with questions about the store's wares. Halfway amused, I found myself wondering if the Millers had posted guards on either side of Full Moon

Apothecary to make sure no one else came in while the three of us were talking.

Judging by the couple's high-handed manner, I wouldn't have been at all surprised if that turned out to be the case.

But even as I patiently answered questions about arthritis tinctures and insomnia elixirs, I felt a stir of unease.

What would the formidable Lorna Miller and her husband do if I failed to dig up any clues regarding their son's murder?

Worse, what would they do if I did?

Chapter 8

A Nose for Crime

The rest of that afternoon, I couldn't help fretting over whether I should tell Noah about the Millers' visit to the shop despite Lorna's comment about our conversation being confidential. I couldn't claim to know much of anything about the two of them, but I got the impression they weren't the sort of people to share their thoughts and feelings with others, and therefore were probably planning to stay silent on the subject unless I actually dug up something that proved to be useful.

So, it would probably be better just to stay quiet. After all, I was already keeping plenty of secrets from Noah—about my witchiness, about what I'd seen in the scrying mirror last night.

But those facts had to be held close to my vest because they involved magic, whereas keeping my mouth shut on the subject of Lorna and Thad Miller felt more like withholding information he should know. After all, what was the worst that would happen if I told Noah they'd paid me a visit this afternoon?

Well, for one thing, he could tell me he didn't think it was a very good idea for me to go anywhere near Miller & Miller, even if it seemed as if the most likely place to pick up information about Trevor that wasn't colored by family loyalty or affection. I knew Noah would never outright forbid me to do something, partly because we hadn't known each other long enough for him to do anything so stupid, but mostly because he simply wasn't the kind of man to demand such a thing of me.

Or at least, I didn't think he was.

I went back and forth with myself, eventually coming to the admittedly wishy-washy decision that I wouldn't say anything on the subject unless he directly brought it up, which didn't seem very likely. This was a coward's way out, probably, because there was no reason for him to believe I'd had any contact with the Millers at all, but I just couldn't think of how else to deal with the situation.

To tell the truth, I didn't even know what I planned to do yet, although the notion had surfaced that I didn't work Sundays and Mondays, and that meant it would be easy enough for me to head down to Boston on Monday and try a little amateur sleuthing around the Millers' architectural firm. The thought of doing anything so brazen wasn't the most appealing thing in the world—I'd never tried to question someone to get background information, not even when screening applicants for the sales assistant position at my store—and yet something was telling me I might find something useful if I was just willing to take the chance.

Well, Monday was a long ways off. I still had to get through dinner with Noah tonight.

Way to make it sound like a root canal or something, I thought sourly as I wrapped up a bottle of my spring tonic for a pale woman with a North Carolina driver's license, someone who definitely looked as though she could use a pick-me-up. *It's a date, not the Spanish Inquisition.*

True enough. I hated keeping things from Noah, though, and so I prayed our meal wouldn't be like a proverbial mine field, with me desperately trying to avoid any topics that might send up red flags. For all I knew, he wouldn't even want to talk about Trevor's murder, and would rather focus on much more pleasant topics, like the planned barbecue at Jared and Kathy's house on Saturday night.

That would make things much easier. I could try to rationalize the situation by telling myself there was no point relaying what had happened between the Millers and me, since I didn't even know for sure whether I was going to head down to Boston on Monday or not, but....

No matter how you looked at it, I was splitting an awful lot of hairs here.

I was glad I'd have a little time at home to decompress before Noah picked me up for dinner, and gladder still to get there and find the two familiars draped over each other on the living room sofa. Because I had familiars coming and going at irregular intervals, I'd long ago decided not to worry about keeping the furniture pristine and had instead decided to go for an aesthetic that at best could be described as "shabby chic."

"Did you have a good day?" I asked, and Cinny stretched before languidly dropping off the couch onto the rug.

"I did," she said, while Milo also stretched and then yawned. "There's something very relaxing about being here."

I'd often thought the same thing, and sometimes wondered if I should cut down the hours I worked during the off season, just so I'd be able to spend more time at home. Whenever I got close to making a decision, though, things at the store would pick up, and I'd decide it was probably better to keep my schedule the way it currently was.

Also, I wasn't too surprised Cinny felt more

relaxed here at the house than she usually did. She had Milo to keep her company, and she didn't have her high-strung mistress around to put her continually on edge.

However, I didn't feel as though I should comment on that subject, especially since Cinny would only be with me for a few more days.

"You might have something there," Milo remarked before he joined Cinnamon on the rug. "Charity, have you ever thought about being a kind of vacation home for familiars, a place where they can come and decompress for a bit?"

I lifted an eyebrow, even as I thought that might be a pretty good idea. It was unusual to have two familiars come stay with me in such quick succession, and I had to admit the house felt kind of empty when I went months at a time without having someone's animal companion around. True, now I had Milo living with me, so I wouldn't be alone when Cinny went back to Doris.

Still...it was something to think about. I knew Milo liked having company, but getting a regular cat or dog wouldn't be the same as having another familiar to hang out with while I was at work. Most of the time, familiars really didn't get to spend a lot of time in one another's company, since they were supposed to be helping their witches and sticking close to them, so I thought the idea had a certain appeal.

Right now, though, I had other things on my plate, and I knew I couldn't really spend much time thinking about this new notion until the investigation into Trevor Miller's death reached some sort of conclusion.

Was I hoping that conclusion would be reached by the Salem P.D., maybe that Detective Falco Lorna had mentioned?

Absolutely. But until then, I knew I had to keep working at it in my own unorthodox way.

"It's a possibility," I said, since both Milo and Cinny were looking at me expectantly, obviously waiting for a reply to his question. "I've got some other stuff going on right now, though, so I probably won't be able to really stop and think about it for a while."

"This new murder investigation?" Milo asked, his tail wagging in excitement.

"Yes," I responded. "But in this case, the victim was a mundie. I don't think it has anything to do with the witch world at all."

The dog immediately looked somewhat crestfallen at my answer. Maybe he was thinking he could jump in and be the hero, just like he had when he took a chunk out of Brian Alatorre's leg when the man-turned-creature attacked me.

While I was heartened by Milo's willingness to play protector, I didn't think there was much he could do here.

Before I could go on, though, Cinny put in, "But couldn't you have Milo sniff around the crime scene? He might be able to tell you which way the killer went."

I wanted to protest that the trail was ice cold by now, with the murderer long gone. Dog's noses were sensitive, though, and those of canine familiars even more so, as if their natural abilities had been enhanced, just like their intelligence.

"Yes, I could do that!" Milo exclaimed at once.

"A lot of people have come and gone in that house since the victim was murdered," I warned him. "You might not be able to smell anything except the tracks the police and their forensics team left behind."

Milo stood up proudly, nose in the air. "I think I would be able to tell the difference."

Maybe he would. It was possible that the people on the forensics team would smell like chemicals, the cops like gunpowder. I didn't have a dog's nose, so I really had no idea what kinds of things he might be able to pick up.

"All right," I said, and glanced at the clock on the mantel. It was a little past five-thirty, and Noah wouldn't be here to pick me up until seven.

Hannah's cottage was only ten minutes away.

That seemed to settle things. I smiled at Milo and said, "Want to go on a field trip?"

* * *

I knew it was all right to go back to the cottage, because Hannah had told me her next guests wouldn't be arriving until the end of the following week. She hadn't said it was okay for me to come and go as I pleased, but I figured a quick trip over there shouldn't be too much of a problem.

After all, it was always better to ask for forgiveness than permission.

There were enough people in the neighborhood coming home from work that I decided it was better to park in the alley behind the cottage and enter the property through the back gate rather than walk in the front door with a cocker spaniel trotting at my side. As we went, Milo sniffed everywhere, but it seemed to me he was just gathering intelligence, since he didn't comment, only followed along as we went up the two steps to the kitchen door.

A quick unlocking spell murmured under my breath, and we were inside. Again, my canine companion started sniffing around, nose almost touching the baseboards and the tile floor.

"Lots of people here," he said after a few moments.

"So, you can't pick anything out?" I asked. It was way too early to feel this disappointed, but I supposed I'd been hoping that Milo's super-tuned nose might have been able to coax out something.

"Not yet," he replied, looking unconcerned. "But I just need to keep going."

I followed him as he nosed his way down the short corridor that separated the kitchen from the living space. Once there, he started sniffing all over the place, while I stood off to one side and hoped that any trail the killer might have left behind hadn't been completely overlaid by the scents of the people who'd come here to investigate the crime.

He paid particular attention to the blood patch on the rug, coming back to it over and over again. At last, he gave a satisfied wag of his tail and said, "I think I've got something."

"Got what?"

Without replying immediately, he sniffed along the rug and partway down the corridor, and stopped again. "Yes, the killer went this way," he said.

I blinked in surprise. "You're sure?"

"Yes," Milo replied without hesitation. "He went down this hallway and..." The words trailed off as he sniffed back into the kitchen, then went on, "He went into the kitchen and down the back stairs."

"It was a he?" I asked then. So much for my admittedly crazy...and less and less plausible...idea that Shelby was the one who'd murdered Trevor and who'd concocted that story about a black-clad ninja-style killer sticking a sword in her fiancé's back.

"Definitely a man," Milo said, again without missing a beat.

I came into the kitchen and opened the back door. At once, the dog hurried out, nose close to the stairs and the path that bisected the cottage's tiny garden. He paused at the gate, and I sped up my steps so I could go over there and open it.

Still with his head low, sniffing, he went to roughly the same spot where my car was parked, then stopped. "The trail ends here," he said, sounding disappointed. "He must have gotten in his car and driven away."

"Do you have any idea which direction he went?" I asked, even as I thought that was asking a bit much of the dog. It was one thing for him to distinguish between different human scents, and quite another for him to track a car or SUV, which probably all smelled the same to him, of exhaust and rubber.

Milo lifted his nose in the air, sniffing. "I'm not sure," he replied, which was pretty much what I'd expected.

"It's all right," I said, and bent down so I could give him a thank-you scratch behind the ears.

"That's still a lot more than I knew a few minutes ago."

"I think he went that way, though," Milo told me, nose pointing south.

Toward Boston?

I reminded myself that there were plenty of towns between Salem and Boston, and the killer could have been headed to any one of them. Still, that Milo seemed to think the murderer had gone south after committing the crime meant I probably should be looking in that direction...whether I liked it or not.

"Good to know," I said, and smiled. "You've helped me a lot, Milo. Now, though, I need to get you home. We don't want to leave Cinny alone for too long."

At once, Milo's tail began to wag. "Yes, she's doing better, but she still likes having me around."

That seemed to be my sign that we were done here. The two of us walked over to the car—well, after I took a brief detour to go to the back door and cast another spell to lock it—and then we both headed for home.

No, I still didn't know who the murderer was, but at least now I knew it was a he, and that he'd probably headed south after leaving that sword sticking out of Trevor's back. That narrowed things down a bit...if not quite as much as I'd hoped.

* * *

Noah and I drove to Marblehead to a brewery there, and for the first part of our meal, everything seemed to go just fine. Neither one of us mentioned anything about Trevor Miller or the murder, instead talking about our days at work and our plans for the weekend, just like any regular couple would.

But after I was partway through my French dip and Noah through his burger, he set it down and gave me a direct look. "Shelby wanted to know if you've had any luck yet," he said.

I wanted to return, "Luck about what?", but knew that kind of disingenuous response probably wouldn't go over very well.

"Not really," I said. "But I'm pretty sure the murderer was male."

Noah's expression brightened. "What makes you say that? From what I've heard so far, the police weren't able to find any DNA evidence on the scene that didn't belong to either Shelby or Trevor."

Where had he gotten that information? As far as I knew, he wasn't buddy-buddy with anyone on the police force.

But maybe Shelby's lawyer had been able to get his hands on that particular detail, and he'd passed it along to his client. Since I hadn't been privy to their conversations, I had no idea.

"Oh, I took Milo over to the cottage," I said, then added as Noah raised an eyebrow, "Hannah said it would be okay. Anyway, he sniffed around and seemed to find a trail from the bloodstain on the rug to the back door."

Looking impressed, Noah settled against the back of his chair and lifted his glass of Hefeweizen. "It's great that he found a trail, but how do you know it belonged to a man?"

"Because of the way he pointed," I replied, thinking furiously. After all, I couldn't very well respond that Milo had simply told me the killer was male. "His former mistress taught him to do that. He points when he's following a trail from a man and wags his tail when it's a woman."

Since Noah knew absolutely nothing about Darla Fitzgerald except that Milo had been her dog and she'd lived in Chicago, he couldn't really question the veracity of my statement. He nodded and said, "That's a handy trick."

"It is," I agreed. "And that's why I thought I should bring Milo over there to check things out. Did the police investigating the murder bring any dogs along to sniff around?"

"Not that I know of," Noah said. "Maybe they decided the trail was too cold by the time they got there."

Thanks to Shelby insisting on speaking to us first before she called the cops. I still didn't know exactly why she'd done that, but it did seem as if she'd been so shaken up, she really hadn't been thinking straight.

"Milo's a very impressive dog," he went on, now smiling a little. "Maybe he should go work for the Salem P.D."

"No, he's staying safe at home with me," I replied at once. Yes, Noah had been mostly joking, but I didn't want him to get the idea that Milo should be a police dog or something. After what he'd been through with Brian Alatorre, he needed to stay far, far out of harm's way.

Noah must have picked up on the note of disapproval in my tone, because he abandoned that subject immediately, instead saying, "So...are you going to tell the police?"

"About the killer being male?"

"Yes."

"I could," I said. "But I'm not sure they'd believe me. After all, I know how good Milo is at this sort of thing, but...."

I didn't bother to finish the sentence. Like all other witches, I did as much as I could to stay out of the orbit of the police, since the last thing I wanted was to attract any attention to myself. If I went to the station and told them my super-talented dog had figured out that Trevor Miller's killer was definitely a man, they probably would have laughed me right out of there...or requested a seventy-two-hour psychiatric hold.

Noah must have been thinking much the same thing, because he didn't press the issue. Instead, he reached for his burger again and asked, "Do you mind if I tell Shelby that? I mean, she already knows she's innocent, but it's something she'd probably want to tell her lawyer. It's something they can keep in their back pocket just in case things go sideways."

"Sure," I said. "But just remember it's probably not anything that would be admissible in court."

"Maybe not," he allowed. "I'll let Shelby's lawyer make the determination on that. But it might help...and it shows you really are trying to do your best to get all this figured out."

At those words, I set down my French dip and sent Noah a narrow glance. "What, did you think I wasn't?"

"Of course not," he replied at once. His mouth tightened a little, although I couldn't tell whether he was irritated with me, or with himself for the way he'd phrased his previous comment. "It's just...." He stopped there, and let out a breath. "Last night, Shelby's mother was kind of on her case, and was saying that Shelby should have hired a private investigator to look into things rather than relying on an amateur. No offense," he added, now with that familiar glint back in his bright blue eyes.

"None taken," I told him, and felt my mouth quirk. "I *am* an amateur. It would have been much better for Shelby to hire someone who knows what they're doing."

"Well, she has faith in you," Noah said. "And so do I. After all, you've already discovered something the police didn't know. I'd say that was pretty good detective work."

"From Milo," I pointed out, and Noah's shoulders lifted.

"True, but you knew what his talents were, and how you could work with them. It still might have made all the difference."

Maybe. I honestly didn't think it was that big a deal, since all I had was a couple of very small leads and nothing more.

So much depended on what I might discover in Boston on Monday...and I couldn't tell Noah anything about that.

Chapter 9

True Confessions

Saturday at work was uneventful, if busy. Doris called not too long after I got home, and her voice was almost plaintive.

"How are things with Cinny?" she asked. "I want to bring her home."

"She's fine," I said. "I think we're working through things. In fact—" I paused, knowing my next suggestion probably wasn't going to go over very well—"in fact, I'd like to keep her with me for a while longer. I think it would do her a lot of good."

"Why do you say that?"

Doris's tone had sharpened, and I knew I needed to tread lightly. No, she wasn't the most congenial person in the world, but she obviously cared about her familiar, and even the whiff of a suggestion that Cinny wasn't completely happy about her home situation wouldn't sit very well.

"She's having a lot of fun being with Milo," I explained. "Sometimes the best thing in the world for a person—or a familiar—is to have a change of scenery, new people to spend time with. Think of it like...like Cinny being on vacation."

That explanation was followed by a long, pregnant pause. I wondered if I should try to say something else, then realized I'd already stuck my foot in it, so I might as well wait for Doris to respond.

"Familiars don't take vacations," she said, sounding even frostier than she had a moment earlier.

"No," I replied. "But maybe they should."

She didn't say anything for a moment. Then I heard a sniff, followed by, "You can have her until Thursday. I absolutely cannot spare her any longer than that."

I guessed it had taken a bit of inner struggle for Doris to give me even those four extra days. Because of that, I only said, "That would be wonderful. Thank you for giving her some extra time with me and Milo."

"Ten o'clock on Thursday morning," Doris intoned. "Not a moment longer. Have her ready to go."

And then I heard an audible *click*, telling me she'd been calling from a landline.

Well, four days was better than nothing. I could only hope that by then, Cinny would have accepted that she wasn't biologically capable of being a mother...and would be ready to go home.

Either way, I had a feeling I needed to let Sage know I would be coming in late on Thursday morning.

* * *

But that Saturday night at Jared and Kathy's house was everything I could have hoped for. Their golden retriever, Lucky, was super-friendly—and obviously disappointed, after smelling Milo's scent on my jeans, that I hadn't brought my dog along with me.

We talked and laughed and ate and drank, and planned another outing on Jared's boat for Sunday of next week. My German potato salad was a huge hit, with the bowl getting scraped clean.

The whole evening, I couldn't stop thinking about how this was how it was supposed to be— just friends getting together, no huge agenda, no hidden witch worlds or crimes that needed to be solved. Maybe other people's lives were always like this, and I found myself suddenly wistful, wondering what my own life would have been like if I hadn't been born into a witch family whose line stretched back hundreds of years.

Not that I really wanted to give up my magic, of course. At the same time, it could get awfully tiring, having to hide such a huge part of yourself from the rest of the world.

"You seem a little quiet," Noah remarked after we'd gotten in his pickup truck and he pulled away from the curb.

I managed a smile. "Just sleepy. All that food and wine and sunshine."

"True...and you worked a full day today. I only had to do four hours at the clinic this morning, and then I was done."

"Well, until Monday morning," I pointed out. At least I got two full days off, whereas Noah's weekend was really just a day and a half long.

"It's all right," he said. "Summers are actually a little quieter for me because of all the people who take their pets with them on vacation."

I hadn't really thought about that, mostly because until I'd inherited Milo, I didn't have an animal around full-time.

Oh, and also because I never really took any extended time off. Those days I'd spent taking care of him after he was wounded had been the longest time I'd spent away from the shop since I'd opened the business more than five years ago.

Noah went on, tone now a little diffident, "I'd say we should get together tomorrow, but Shelby and her mom want to take me out to brunch to say thanks for my help."

Once again, I couldn't help thinking that I'd been the one doing most of the work. But I gave a forced chuckle that probably wouldn't have fooled anyone and said, "Oh, that's fine. Sunday's laundry day for me, anyway."

For a moment, Noah didn't reply, only waited until he was able to turn the corner and merge into traffic. Not looking at me, he said, "Are you upset about the time I'm spending with Shelby?"

"Of course not," I replied at once, even if I wasn't sure whether that was entirely the truth. "She's in trouble, and obviously, she's going to reach out to the people she knows to give her support right now."

That sounded very noble. No, I wasn't exactly jealous of Shelby...even if she had the picture-perfect girl-next-door kind of looks I'd always secretly envied...but I also didn't like her taking up so much of Noah's headspace when our relationship was still so new and fragile.

"I never told you why we broke up, did I?" he ventured next, and I sent him a surprised look.

"No," I replied. "I mean, I didn't ask. I figured it wasn't any of my business."

"Her family has a lot of money," he said. "I only mention that because I think it was part of the problem between us. My own family's pretty solidly middle class—my dad's an electrician, and my mother owns a hair salon—and although my parents do okay, they're not exactly the kind of people who have a vacation home in the Hamptons."

"That's okay," I said with a smile. "Neither are mine."

"No, you seem pretty down to earth," he said. "And I appreciate that."

I could feel my cheeks warm, and was glad it was now past dusk so he couldn't see the betraying flush. At the same time, my mouth quirked just a bit, and I wondered if he would have described me that way if he'd known I was a witch.

"Anyway, Shelby's and my orbits would never have even crossed if I hadn't met her at a party thrown by a guy I was going to vet school with. His family was also pretty wealthy, and he knew Shelby from college. Long story short, she and I started dating, and after I got my degree, I started working at one of the top vet clinics in Boston." Noah stopped there, now looking almost shame-faced. "Shelby swore up and down that her family had nothing to do with me getting that job, but I'm still not sure whether I really believe her or not. Anyway, we dated for about two years, and then we got engaged. The engagement lasted a year and a half."

"Her family didn't approve?" I asked. I didn't

think the question was too out of line, considering he'd said only a few minutes earlier that Shelby's family's money had something to do with the breakup.

"No, they liked me," Noah said. "Or at least, they acted like they did. I think they all assumed I'd stay at that clinic until Dr. Hawthorne retired, and then they'd help me buy the practice and could tell everyone that their son-in-law owned one of the top vet clinics in Boston."

I slid him a sideways glance. We'd just turned onto Winter Island Drive, so his attention was on the road, but I got the feeling he was glad to have a reason to face forward so he wouldn't have to look at me.

"And that wasn't what you wanted?"

He chuckled. "Obviously not, or I wouldn't be here in Salem."

After that, he went quiet for a moment, since it was time to angle his truck into my driveway. Once he came to a stop and put the vehicle in park, he apparently decided it was okay for him to go on with his narrative.

"I was already feeling restless. It would prob-ably have been another ten years before Dr. Hawthorne retired, and I knew I didn't want to stay in Boston that long. I told Shelby I wanted to move, wanted to get out of the big city and set up my practice someplace smaller and friendlier."

"I'm assuming that didn't go over too well," I said dryly.

"That's an understatement. She got angry and told me a relationship was more than one person deciding what they wanted, and I said yes, that was true, and that was why I wanted to talk to her about it. She said she absolutely wasn't leaving Boston and that I needed to pay more attention to what she wanted." Noah paused there, and now he shifted so he was facing me. His expression was calm enough, maybe even a little ruefully amused, but I guessed telling me all this still wasn't easy for him. "Then I asked her if she'd ever be able to compromise, and she told me no, that we'd gotten engaged in Boston and I'd never given her the slightest hint that I wanted to live somewhere else. She said I wasn't being fair."

"You tried to talk to her," I said quietly, and he shrugged.

"I did. But sometimes it's impossible to meet halfway. I knew I'd be miserable if I stayed in Boston, and I didn't see any way out. Of course, she took the final step—called things off, returned the ring I bought her." He gave me a lopsided smile. "I guess I can be glad about that part, because I was already trying to pay off my student debt and was able to get a friend to sell the ring on eBay for me."

Silver linings, I supposed. I'd already guessed

that Noah was probably still dealing with paying off his loans, because regular college was already expensive enough without adding a DVM degree to the mix. True, he'd probably gotten grants and things for part of it, but I had a feeling that was why he was driving an eight-year-old truck and didn't seem too extravagant. His house was nice, but definitely not a mansion or anything, and I still had no idea whether he owned the place or was only renting it.

And I liked that about him. I liked that he was just an ordinary guy—all right, an extremely gorgeous ordinary guy—and I was just an ordinary woman.

Well, except for that whole witch thing.

"So, that's the whole sad story," he concluded. "I suppose maybe I still feel a little guilty about the way things ended with Shelby, and that's why I'm trying to give her some support now. It's been completely over between us for a while...and maybe even longer than I originally thought, considering how quickly she hooked up with Trevor after the two of us split...but that doesn't mean I can't still be a friend to her."

"I think it's amazing," I said honestly. "And I'll do whatever I can to help."

"I know you will," he said, his tone now softer as his eyes met mine. "Because you're amazing as well."

Those were the last words spoken for quite a while. After he wished me goodnight, I hurried inside, wondering if any of my neighbors had seen the two of us making out in the front seat of his truck like a couple of high school kids trying to avoid getting caught by their parents.

Not that it mattered. I definitely wasn't in high school anymore, and neither was Noah. And now that he'd cleared the air and I knew he absolutely didn't have any feelings for Shelby beyond friendship, I had to admit my outlook on the whole situation was a lot sunnier than it had been even a few hours earlier.

Now all I had to do was figure out who really had killed Trevor Miller, and Shelby and her mother could go back to Boston...and be out of Noah's and my hair forever.

Chapter 10

What Happens in Boston

I t was less than an hour from Salem to Boston, but I still wasn't looking forward to the drive. These days, I didn't leave my hometown very often...I couldn't count a jaunt over to Marblehead as exactly leaving my neck of the woods...and I had to admit my fingers gripped the steering wheel a little more tightly than they probably should as I turned off Highway 128 onto Highway 1, heading south.

Then again, my trepidation might have stemmed more from my unease about concealing this trip from Noah than worries about Boston traffic. Yes, I could tell myself over and over again until I was blue in the face that there was no way I could possibly explain how I knew my investigation needed to go in this direction without revealing how I'd used magic to get to this point, but those excuses rang pretty hollow.

He deserved better.

But you can't say anything, I thought, as if scolding myself in that firm, no-nonsense mental voice might somehow make me feel better about the situation. *You haven't known him long enough to tell him the truth.*

Even that excuse didn't feel quite right. True, Noah and I had only been romantically involved for less than two weeks, but we'd known each other for almost a year. Shouldn't that count for something?

Possibly, and yet I realized deep down it still wasn't enough.

The green Massachusetts countryside rolled past as I traveled south, but I knew I wasn't in any mood to appreciate its beauty.

No, I just wanted to get this trip over with as quickly as possible and head straight back to Salem, where I could at least let my guard down when I was home. Milo and Cinny knew I needed to make this trip to see if I could find any more clues that pointed to Trevor Miller's murderer, and they'd assured me they'd be just fine spending a few hours home alone on what should have been one of my days off with them. True, we'd had all day Sunday together, and Cinnamon had seemed much more cheerful, as though she was getting used to the reality of her kitten-less state.

All the same, I was very glad I'd convinced Doris that her familiar should stay with me a bit longer than the original seven days we'd agreed upon.

Boston was as crowded and hectic as ever, and I knew I must have annoyed quite a few motorists with my granny-style, cautious driving. But since I wasn't as familiar with the city as I knew I should be, it just seemed safer to take it slow until I finally reached the parking garage about halfway down the street from the impressive building where Miller & Miller was located.

As I approached the front entrance, I found myself wondering if the original Miller had designed the place. It was newer than some of the other downtown buildings, clearly dating to the 1800s rather than the eighteenth century or even earlier, and was handsome brick with an elaborate cornice and moldings around the huge double doors that led into the lobby.

During my drive, I'd decided the best thing to do was pretend to be a walk-in client and see if anyone would take an impromptu meeting with me. Maybe it was silly to be so off-the-cuff about the whole situation, but since I'd made my final decision about coming here over the weekend, it wasn't as though I would have been able to call and make an appointment anyway.

Although other businesses also occupied the building, the Millers' architectural firm took up the entire top two floors. Luckily, the directory I stopped to check as I entered the lobby told me the reception area was on the fourth floor, so at least I wouldn't have to worry about showing up in the wrong place.

Just like down in the lobby, the open area right outside the elevator had patterned marble floors, although the original woodwork here had been painted a soft dove gray, with the walls a cool white. The effect was an interesting mix of Victorian and modern, and probably a nod toward letting the firm's clients know that its design sense was firmly fixed in the here and now despite how long it had been in existence.

The reception area was located behind a set of double doors. I pushed through into another white and gray space, softened by large fiddle-leaf fig plants in washed concrete planters placed at strategic intervals. Sitting at a large white oak and steel desk directly in front of me was a woman who looked as though she was probably in her mid-thirties, a few years older than I. Her fair hair was slicked back into a sleek ponytail, and she wore a sleeveless silk blouse in a cool blue shade that echoed the color of her eyes.

Even though I'd done my best to make myself look respectable for this visit and had worn one of my few tops that wasn't black and the only pair of dress pants I owned, I couldn't help feeling a little intimidated by the receptionist's polished perfection. If she was this put together, what would the actual architects look like?

I told myself I hadn't driven all the way down here only to turn tail and run, and made myself step a little closer to the desk.

"Can I help you?" the woman asked. She didn't have a single trace of a New England accent, and I wondered if she was from somewhere else in the United States, or had just made sure to erase any sign of her origins from her voice.

"Hi," I said, glad I sounded mostly relaxed. "My name is Charity Hughes. I don't have an appointment, but I was wondering if I could talk to one of your architects. I'm thinking of remodeling my business."

Well, that was the story I'd concocted to explain why I wanted to speak with someone at the firm, anyway.

The woman, who'd been wearing an expression that bordered on dubious but hadn't quite made it all the way there, brightened a little. "We don't usually see people without appointments," she told me.

"I'm really sorry," I said. "I was down in

Boston for the day and realized this was probably my best chance to find someone to work with. My business is in Salem," I added, "and I haven't been happy with any of the design ideas I've gotten from our local architects."

Obviously, that was a blatant lie. But if she bought it, well, I'd just tell myself that in this particular case, the ends definitely justified the means.

The receptionist's expression shifted subtly. Was she thinking this might be a good chance to show me what a big city firm could do on my project?

Apparently so, because she said, "Let me see if one of our associates is available. Can you wait a moment?"

And she nodded toward a group of four gray-upholstered parsons chairs clustered near a marble and glass coffee table.

"Sure," I said, and hurried over to the waiting area and sat down.

She picked up her phone and made what looked like a couple of quick calls. After the last one, she set the handset in the receiver and sent me a smile. "One of our associates if free. Let me take you to his office."

Thank God.

I stood up as she came out from behind her desk. However, she didn't lead me to the double doors behind her, which I assumed opened onto offices or maybe a cube farm, depending on how the business was set up, but back over to the elevators. We took one to the fifth floor, and then she guided me through an equally gray but this time empty reception area and down a hall toward an office at the end.

"You're in luck," she told me as we walked. "Bryce Foster just finished up a big project, so he has some time to talk to you. He's one of our up-and-coming associates."

It seemed that way, since it turned out his office was located on the corner and had a commanding view of downtown Boston and the Charles River. As soon as the receptionist guided me in, Bryce got up from behind his desk and extended a hand, saying, "Nice to meet you, Ms. Hughes."

"Thank you for seeing me without an appointment," I replied.

He shrugged, then glanced over at the receptionist. "Thanks for bringing her up here, Siobhan."

The receptionist nodded, then stepped out, closing the office door behind her.

I looked back at Bryce. He was probably around my age, maybe a year or two older, with sandy hair and brown eyes and friendly, almost boyish features.

"What can I do for you, Ms. Hughes?" he asked.

"Charity," I said quickly.

He smiled. "All right, Charity. Siobhan said you were thinking of remodeling your business. What kind of business is it?"

"I have a shop in downtown Salem, on Essex Street," I explained. "It's kind of an apothecary store. I'd really like to do something to brighten it up and allow for a better shopping experience."

"Do you have any pictures?"

"I do," I replied, glad that the snaps I'd taken of the store after I'd rearranged the displays a year earlier were still on my phone. "They're not the greatest in the world, but I hope they'll show you what I mean."

A moment while I fished my iPhone out of my purse and scrolled through my photos, and then I handed the phone over to Bryce.

He studied the images displayed there for a moment, then nodded. "Is the building a single story?"

"Yes," I said. Not for the first time, I wished the building my shop occupied had more than one floor, because that way, I probably could have stored more stock there.

"Have you thought about skylights?"

To be honest, the notion had never even

entered my mind. But I supposed that was why you consulted an architect in the first place.

"No," I said, and he smiled.

"That would be a simple way to get more natural light into the space," Bryce explained. "Any other issues you'd like to have addressed?"

What I really wanted was to ask him what he thought about Trevor Miller, whether the man had any enemies, professional or otherwise, but I knew now wasn't the time. No, I needed to keep easing the conversation along and hope I could find an opening where I could broach the subject that was the real reason for my being here.

"I'd really like more storage," I said. "I've rearranged things what feels like a hundred times, but there's never enough space."

Bryce flipped back and forth amongst the photos of the shop, brows pulling together. He wore a gold band on the ring finger of his left hand, telling me he must be married. Was this his first job after getting his architect certification, or had he landed here recently? Under normal circumstances, I wouldn't really care one way or another, but if he hadn't been at Miller & Miller for very long, he might not know that much about Trevor.

"It looks like you might have room to extend the back of the shop another two or three feet," Bryce said. "I know that might not sound like much, but it could do a lot, especially when you pair a better storage system with those extra couple of feet. Would the city allow you to do that?"

I actually knew the answer to that question, because I'd thought pretty much the same thing and had explored the idea with Salem's planning department, then had abandoned the project as being a little too expensive for me at the moment.

"Yes, I think so," I said. "I'd have to check to be sure, but I know other shop owners in the same block have done it, so I think it should be okay."

"Well, then," Bryce said with another smile. "I'd need to come to the site to give you a firm estimate. Would you like to schedule an appointment?"

I could only imagine what Noah's reaction would be if he discovered that an architect from Trevor's firm had showed up at Full Moon Apothecary and gotten out his tape measure, or whatever he needed to give me a quote on the project. "Um...I'm kind of fact finding right now," I told him, one of the few truthful things I'd uttered during our entire interview. "To be honest, I probably wouldn't want to get started on the project until after the first of the year. Summer through autumn is our busiest time in Salem."

Although I'd halfway expected Bryce to be irritated by the way I'd just backpedaled the project, instead he just nodded. "I can see that. Having your store torn up wouldn't give your customers a very good shopping experience."

"No, it wouldn't," I agreed. "But I figured it would still be a good idea to see if updating the space was even feasible. The building is pretty old." I paused there, guessing that if I didn't start heading this conversation in the right direction soon, I'd be back in my car on the way home to Salem with nothing to show for my efforts except a wasted day off. "Probably older than this one," I went on. "Was it built by the Millers?"

"Yes," Bryce replied. He didn't seem put off by the question, and went on, "Norbert Miller built it back in 1882. The firm has been here ever since. I feel really lucky that I was able to land a position here right after college."

I wanted to let out an exhalation of relief but wouldn't allow myself. So, Bryce had been here at the firm for a while, probably at least five or six years, maybe more. That meant he had to have known Trevor, even if they might not have worked together directly.

"Yes, Miller & Miller has a great reputation," I said. "That's why I wanted to get a quote from your company, even though I know mine is a small project compared to most. But the city of Salem requires an architect to sign off on any alterations because of the age of my building."

I stopped there.

Now or never.

"It's really awful what happened," I went on. "With Trevor Miller, I mean."

At once, Bryce's expression grew sober, although I didn't see any wariness in his face, anything to tell me he was on his guard about the direction our conversation had taken. "I know," he said. "We're all still in shock here."

"Did you work with him a lot?"

"Not really," Bryce replied, still with the air of someone who was only passing on information and who didn't seem to sense there might be an ulterior motive behind the questions I was asking. "I mean, he's a partner, and I'm just an associate. A senior associate," he added quickly, as if he wanted to assure me that I hadn't been handed over to a rank amateur for my dinky remodeling gig, "but still, he tended to work on the bigger projects. He was really talented."

And then Bryce released a breath, as if thinking of all the buildings Trevor would never be able to design, all the structures that would now never exist because he'd been cut down in the prime of life.

I hoped I looked appropriately sad as well. The whole thing was a tragedy, and, more than ever, I wanted to figure out who in the world could have done such an awful thing.

"There was something about a sword?" I prompted.

Bryce looked a little startled by that question, but then appeared to tell himself that I'd probably heard all about it in the local paper. "Yes, that was the weird thing. Trevor was really into fencing when he went to Yale, and he started collecting antique swords around the same time. He had a couple of them hanging in his office here, and I guess one of them was taken and...well, was used in the crime."

None of that was anything I hadn't heard before. "Do you have any idea how it could have been stolen?"

Now Bryce's eyes narrowed a bit, as if he'd finally realized this line of questioning didn't have a thing to do with remodeling a shop in a historic building in Salem. "No," he said, his tone much more abrupt than it had been a moment earlier. "Nobody does. The custodial staff swears up and down that everything was locked up tight, and there's nothing on any of the security cameras that shows the sword being taken. But that's all anyone knows." He stopped there, sandy brows lifting a bit. Wearing a very faint smile, he went on, "You don't really need to have your shop remodeled, do you? What are you, a reporter?"

"You got me," I said with a smile, knowing I needed to bluff my way through this as best I could. "I mean," I added hastily, since like an idiot, I'd given Bryce my real name and it wouldn't be too hard to figure out that I wasn't an actual journalist, "I don't work for a local paper or anything. I'm working on putting together a true-crime blog that focuses on things that have happened in and around Salem."

I purposely phrased it that way so he couldn't ask me for the name of the blog or its URL. If it didn't exist yet, there wasn't anything I'd have to show him.

Bryce didn't say anything for a moment, only sat there on the other side of his desk, eyebrows tilted, hands folded on the knee of his tropical-weight wool slacks. When he spoke, his words startled me.

"Can I speak to you in confidence?"

I stared back at him, then nodded. "Absolutely. Anything I put in the blog will be attributed to an anonymous source."

Actually, Bryce would be even more protected than that, since there wasn't a blog, and I was gathering information for a completely different purpose.

My words seemed to have reassured Bryce, though, because he shifted in his chair, now leaning back, looking a little more relaxed.

"No one could stand the guy," he said.

I blinked. "Trevor Miller?"

Not that Bryce really could have been referring to anyone else, but I figured I'd better get all this straight from the beginning.

"Yes. The guy could barely draw a pediment, let alone design a building, but he got the top spot here at the firm as soon as he graduated. And I'm sure a lot of money changed hands to make sure Trevor got that B. Arch. Most of the rest of us have a master's degree," he added, "but I guess Daddy couldn't grease as many palms in a graduate program."

Interesting. "So...his dad gave him the job because their family owns the firm."

"Exactly," Bryce responded. "I mean, they were always careful to have people on his team who could fix his mistakes, but he still got the credit for everything. The only reason we didn't have associates leaving right and left was because Thad made sure they were paid better than they would have been at any other architectural firms in town."

"Thad?" I asked, even though I knew exactly who the man was. Still, I wanted to continue giving the impression that I didn't know much about the Millers.

"Trevor's father. He's actually a very good architect. I suppose it crushed him to realize his precious son wasn't fit to carry on the family business."

That would have been difficult to deal with.

Not for the first time, I wondered what my mother would have done if I hadn't been born with the Hughes family magic. Tradition stated that I would have been sent off to live with relatives who also had been unfortunate to miss out on inheriting that special magical gene...or whatever it was that gave witches their powers...but because magic had never skipped a generation in the Hughes family the way it sometimes did in others, I honestly had no idea who I would have even gone to live with.

Anyway, it had to be rough to realize that your offspring didn't have your same talents, your same drive.

"Does Thad Miller have any other children?" I asked.

"He has a daughter," Bryce replied. "She's a couple of years younger than Trevor. I guess she's an artist of some kind."

Even though I knew fine art drawing and architectural drawing were two very different things, I couldn't help wondering why the formidable Thad hadn't urged his daughter to become a part of the family business, since at least it sounded as though she had some kind of aptitude.

"She didn't want to join the firm?"

That question made Bryce give a humorless chuckle. "Not while Thad was running things. It might not say 'Miller & Son' on the company letterhead, but he's always been very clear about wanting Trevor and not Amelia as part of the firm."

It sounded to me as though Thad Miller was a real ass, although he'd been impassive enough when he visited my shop in the company of his wife. Then again, I didn't know the whole story. Maybe Trevor's sister Amelia had never wanted anything to do with Miller & Miller, and had preferred to strike out on her own.

"Anyway," Bryce went on, "Trevor's murder might have been a shock to all of us, but it's not as though anyone here is weeping bitter tears over it, either. With him gone, we can stop playing babysitter...and maybe the people who deserve it most will get promoted to senior architect or maybe even partner."

Wow, for someone with such a friendly face, Bryce sure had a cold way of looking at a situation. I tried to be somewhat empathetic, since I'd never had to work at a big corporate job, never had to worry about sucking up to the boss so I could be made partner, or whatever.

All the same, I found myself wondering if Bryce himself could be the killer. He certainly seemed to have held a grudge against Trevor, and maybe he'd decided his only real chance at advancement in his job was to take out the one thing he thought was standing in his way, namely, the boss's son.

I told myself that was silly, that if he really had stabbed Trevor in the back...literally...then he wouldn't be sitting here and telling me about what a waste of oxygen his rival had been.

Or maybe Bryce was relating all this stuff precisely because he wanted me to think no rational person would tell a complete stranger all the reasons why the world was a better place now that Trevor Miller was dead.

My head hurt.

Low blood sugar, probably.

Doing my best to remain as expressionless as I could, I said, "So...do you think anyone here at the firm had a reason to get rid of him?"

Bryce rubbed a hand over the knee of his pants. "Oh, a bunch of people had plenty of reasons. That doesn't mean they did it, though. I imagine you'd need to be pretty pissed off at someone to have the balls to stick a sword in their back."

I'd thought the same thing not too long ago, so I couldn't really argue with that assessment. Still....

"So, you don't think anyone here would be capable of that level of violence?"

He made a sound that was almost a snort. "No way. We're a bunch of desk jockeys, pretty much. About the most you can expect of any of us it a spirited argument about who stole the last K-cup of Irish Cream from the break room."

Despite myself, I smiled. "Okay, point taken."

"Anyway," Bryce went on, "a couple of detectives from your police department already were here and interviewed a bunch of us. I think they were mostly trying to figure out how the sword was stolen from Trevor's office, but they did ask a few questions about the work environment, that kind of thing."

So, I wasn't the only one who'd wondered if the murder had something to do with Trevor's place of work. Too bad I didn't have any real contacts inside the Salem P.D. There was one deputy, Mike Travers, who'd been a year ahead of me in high school, but since he'd been a massive jock and I'd been the oddball redhead who sat in the back of the room and drew sketches of herbs and flowers in the borders of her notebook, we'd never had much to do with one another.

I had a feeling if I reached out to Mike for a chat, he'd immediately suspect I was trying to dig some information out of him, especially if he knew I was currently dating the murder suspect's ex-fiancé.

Either way, it sounded as if Trevor's co-workers were kind of a dead end. Too bad, because it would have been a lot easier to pin the whole thing on professional jealousy and nothing more.

Had this trip been a complete waste of time?

Not really, because at least now I knew Trevor

hadn't been quite the *wunderkind* that Shelby and his own family had made him out to be.

I put on a smile and said, "Well, this has been really interesting, Bryce. Thanks for being so honest with me."

His shoulders lifted. "No problem. Actually, it's been kind of nice to bitch about Trevor to someone other than my wife. She keeps telling me I should just look for another job, but the pay here is too good to pass up. And now with Trevor gone...."

He didn't complete the sentence, but I got the picture. With the boss's son murdered and no one else from the family who could step into his shoes, Bryce finally had the chance for some real advancement in the firm.

Not for the first time, I thanked God and the universe and any other powers out there that I owned my own business. Yes, sometimes it was hard knowing the ultimate responsibility for Full Moon Apothecary's success rested on my shoulders, but on the other hand, I didn't have to worry about cutthroat office politics.

"Thanks so much for taking the time to talk to me," I said, and rose from my chair. Bryce stood up as well, and extended a hand.

"And none of this leaves this room, right?"

"None at all," I assured him.

He seemed to take my words at face value,

because he didn't press the issue, only led me back to the elevators and wished me a good day.

I headed down to the lobby and then went to retrieve my car from the parking garage. Once I put the key in the ignition, I paused for a moment to ponder whether I wanted to run any errands while I was here in town, and ultimately decided against it. There wasn't anything I really needed, and Milo and Cinny were waiting for me at home. If I left now, I'd still have most of the afternoon to spend with them.

As I maneuvered out of the garage, though, I found myself frowning. Had Bryce's story given me anything at all to work with?

For the moment, I didn't think so. It was interesting that Trevor had turned out to be such a crappy architect, but as far as I could tell, that knowledge hadn't changed anything at all.

I blew out a breath, and pointed my Land Rover toward the highway.

Time to go home.

Chapter 11

Special Delivery

When I got back to the house, Milo and Cinny were both sunning themselves out in the backyard, and seemed perfectly content with their lot. Yes, they perked up a little when I told them I was going to throw together some chicken salad for a late lunch, but otherwise, I could tell they would have been just fine if I'd stayed away longer.

Unfortunately, there didn't seem to be much else I could have done in Boston. I wasn't a cop or a private detective, and probably had been asking all the wrong questions. Now I was really glad I hadn't told Noah about my little expedition, because it seemed as if I hadn't gathered a single piece of useful intelligence regarding Trevor Miller's murderer.

I hadn't heard from Noah, and hadn't really

expected to. When he was at work, he was busy, and since we'd kind of left our plans open-ended after seeing each other on Saturday night, there wasn't much need to send a text unless he decided at the last minute that he wanted to get together for takeout or something.

Still, I would have liked to know what he and Shelby and Shelby's mother had discussed during their brunch on Sunday. Maybe he felt anything they talked about was spoken in confidence, and therefore he couldn't have shared it with me even if he'd wanted to. And sure, I supposed I could have been the one to reach out, but I didn't want to come off as too needy, as the kind of woman who couldn't go a couple of days not seeing the man she'd been dating without freaking out that he wasn't that into her.

I knew that wasn't the case. The kisses we'd shared so far told me our chemistry was pretty damn combustible, even if neither one of us had pushed to take the inevitable next step.

Or maybe it wasn't inevitable. For all I knew, the radio silence was his way of telling me he thought we needed to back off a little.

My brain hummed away as I mixed up the chicken salad—and made sure to put a couple of tasty morsels in both Milo and Cinnamon's bowls. They watched me the whole time but obviously could tell I was preoccupied, because neither one of them seemed inclined to chat.

Just as well. I definitely wasn't in the mood to discuss my relationship woes with a couple of familiars, no matter how personable they might be.

After I had lunch and cleaned up the kitchen, I headed into the living room with a notepad and pen, thinking I might as well jot down all the bits and pieces I'd collected regarding Trevor Miller's murder. I kind of doubted I'd come up with anything coherent, but sometimes just writing things out helped to organize my thoughts.

Cinny followed me and promptly curled up on the rug in front of the hearth, although Milo headed outside for a post-lunch bathroom break. The cat didn't seem too curious about what I was doing, and I was fine with that. It was good enough just to have her company, even though a pang went through me as I realized she wouldn't be with me three days from now. No, by Thursday afternoon, Doris would have already come by to collect her familiar.

Since there wasn't anything I could do about that, I told myself to enjoy the time I had left with Cinnamon, and to be here if she wanted to talk. Oddly, after her visit with Noah, she really hadn't brought up the subject of kittens, as if the concrete evidence she'd been given was enough to tell her she wouldn't be able to have a family of her own. A human woman in a similar situation might have started exploring fertility treatments or adoption, but neither of those were really options for Cinny.

Pen in one hand and my notepad on the coffee table, I started scribbling down everything I knew about Trevor's death—where it had happened, the approximate time, the weapon used. Milo's insistence that the killer was a man, someone who'd left the house through the back door and escaped via the alley. That scenario made some sense; the cottage had a detached one-car garage, but Hannah used it to store overflow items from the vacation home and never allowed anyone to rent it out. She expected her guests to park on the street, which meant it was likely that neither Trevor nor Shelby had had any reason to go back there.

I found myself wondering what the reason was for the couple's temporary split. Shelby had said they'd argued, but she hadn't said about what. Maybe that was none of my business, and yet I couldn't help being curious. It couldn't have been too earth-shattering, because they seemed to have reconciled right before his death, but....

Talk to Shelby, I wrote, and then scribbled in a couple of question marks after that. There was every chance in the world that she'd tell me their differences were a private matter and didn't have anything to do with his death.

Then there were Trevor's parents. I assumed

they were already back in Boston, since they'd made it sound as though they only planned to be in Salem long enough to make arrangements for his body to be sent home, but still, they were probably expecting an update from me at some point.

Well, I'd gathered some interesting information today, but I kind of doubted it was the sort of thing either one of them would want to hear.

Cinny appeared to have gone to sleep, so I allowed myself a sigh. It was probably stupid and irresponsible of me to have taken on this case at all, considering I didn't have a clue what I was doing and was basically blundering around in the dark. I thought of the card Lorna had given me, and wondered what she would say if I called her and told her I was stepping away from the whole mess, that I was in way over my head and she really needed to consult a professional. So what if I'd managed to figure out that Brian Alatorre had killed Darla Fitzgerald and kidnapped Milo? It didn't mean I'd be able to do the same thing with an entirely different case.

Just as I was pondering the wisdom of a call to Ms. Miller, my phone—which I'd brought with me after I left the kitchen—began to ring. I reached for it, foolishly hoping that might be Noah, even though we usually communicated via text.

But no, that wasn't his number on the screen.

It was my mother's.

"Hi, Mom," I said, hoping I didn't sound too disappointed. After all, it wasn't as though this call was completely unprecedented, since she often called me on my day off. "What's up?"

"Stella just had her baby!"

My friend Stella Monroe was another witch, someone I'd known pretty much my entire life. We hadn't been quite as close these past couple of years, just because our separate lives had taken us in different directions—especially after she married Kai Ulfsen, a frost elf, a year earlier—but she'd helped me when Milo was dognapped, and because I'd seen her recently, I knew she wasn't due for another month.

"I thought she was supposed to have the baby in July," I said.

"She was," my mother replied. "But babies come when they want, I suppose. Also, Kai told me that frost elves only carry their children for six months, so I guess we should all be glad that Stella's baby was just a month early."

"How are they?"

"Mom and baby are doing fine," my mother told me. "Valerie says it happened so fast that Kai and Stella were barely able to make it to the hospital in time. She can have visitors, so you should really try to drop in and say hi."

This was phrased as a suggestion, but I knew it was more of a command. There weren't so many of us witches in Salem that we could ignore the birth of another of our own. Also, this was the first time in history that a frost elf had had a child with a human, so that was one very special baby.

All the same, I didn't know if I was really looking forward to making such a visit. I was happy for Stella, of course, but with my own personal life kind of up in the air at the moment, I didn't know whether I'd be able to muster the proper enthusiasm.

However, I knew I'd end up going, mostly because my mother would never let me hear the end of it if I didn't...especially since Stella had been so accommodating as to give birth on my day off.

"I'm working on something right now," I said, which wasn't even a lie. "But I'll go over in an hour or so."

"That would be wonderful," my mother replied. "Make sure you bring flowers."

And after assuring my mom that I would get the prettiest bouquet I could find, we ended the conversation. I set the phone back down on the coffee table and frowned at the scribble of notes I'd written right before my mother called. Looking at them now, they seemed like a pretty pitiful collection, and once again I had the urge to contact Lorna Miller and tell her she really needed to get someone else to solve the mystery of her son's murder.

Reason prevailed, though. Instead, I picked up my notepad and pen and stowed them both in one of the coffee table's drawers, pushing aside the deck of Tarot cards I also kept there, then got up from the couch.

Looked like it was time to go flower shopping.

Blue was Stella's favorite color, so I made sure the arrangement I got had some gorgeous blue hydrangeas mixed in with the pink roses and lilies and assorted greenery. Under other circumstances, I might have chosen blue flowers because the baby was a boy, but I knew that wouldn't be the case here. Witches never had male children, and after learning about Brian Alatorre's awful shape-changing secret, I completely understood why.

When I was directed toward Stella's room at the hospital, I passed Grace Bowersby going in the other direction, all smiles. However, she paused when she spotted me, saying, "Oh, Stella will be so glad to see you!"

"How are they doing?" I asked, even though I already knew the answer. It just seemed the correct thing to say.

"Fine, just fine," Grace said. "An easy birth, especially for a first child." She paused there, and added, "Speaking of children, I've been reading through my library, and I haven't found a single instance of a familiar having offspring. I was waiting to contact you until I thought I'd done an exhaustive search, but it really doesn't seem as if my findings are going to change much."

"That's all right," I told her. "I don't think they're physically capable of having them." A glance around told me that, while no one seemed to be paying much attention to our conversation, it still probably wasn't wise to be discussing such a sensitive topic in a busy maternity ward. "But we can talk about that later."

Grace gave me a knowing nod. "I completely understand. Just let me know when you're free to chat."

I promised her I would, then continued toward the room my mother had told me was Stella's. A peek inside revealed my friend lying in bed, a pink-swaddled baby in her arms. Even from where I stood in the doorway, I could see the infant's hair was thick and bright blonde, somewhere between Stella's honey shades and Kai's silver-white locks.

"Hey, there," I said softly, then took a step inside. "How are you doing?"

"Perfect," Stella replied. "Absolutely perfect. And so is she."

She pulled the blanket away from the baby's face so I could get a better look. Even though a lot of children made their entrance to this world red-faced and screaming, the tiny girl's features were instead porcelain perfect, looking almost more like a doll than a human child.

Well, she's not completely human, I reminded myself. *That's a little half-elf you're looking at.*

Speaking of elves....

"Where's Kai?" I asked.

Stella smiled. For someone who'd pushed out a baby only a few hours earlier, she looked absolutely radiant, and not tired at all. "Oh, he went to get me some water. This whole thing wasn't nearly as hard as I thought it might be, but I'm still awfully thirsty."

As if that exchange had summoned him, Kai appeared in the hallway behind me, a cheerful yellow plastic cup in one hand. "Hello, Charity," he said. "It's so kind of you to stop by."

No way in the world would I tell him I never would have heard the end of it if I hadn't. Kai was one of the kindest, most thoughtful people I'd ever met. As far as I'd been able to determine, nothing seemed to ruffle him, and he was never motivated by jealousy or anger or even simple irritation.

"Well, how could I miss out on seeing Salem's newest addition?" I replied with a smile, then moved a little farther into the room, stepping out of the doorway so he could take the cup of water to his wife.

After he handed off the cup, he bent and kissed

Stella on the cheek, then laid another reverent kiss on top of his newborn daughter's head. Watching him, an odd little pang went through me, something almost like longing.

Of course I didn't want Kai to kiss me. He was absolutely devoted to his wife, and I knew the thought of infidelity would never even enter his head.

No, it was more that seeing the three of them together made me want to seriously question my life choices.

I cleared my throat. "So, how long are you going to be in the hospital?"

Stella had been sipping from her cup when I asked the question, so I had to wait a second or two for her to finish before she could reply. "They say I should be able to go home tomorrow, since Aurora and I are both doing fine."

"'Aurora'?" I repeated. "That's her name?"

Kai nodded. "Yes, she was born right after the sun came up, so we thought it would be a good name for her."

"It's lovely."

And it was, a name that suited such a delicate beauty of a child.

We chatted a bit then, with Kai and Stella talking about some of the other names they'd considered, and Stella asking me to come by the house in a few days.

"I think I'll need that long to get adjusted," she said with a smile. "Aurora already seems like she's going to be a champion sleeper, but still, I think I'm going to need a little while to get used to how much things have changed now that she's here."

I could only imagine. Not long after Stella and Kai got together, they'd bought an adorable saltbox Colonial house over on Fairfield Street and had spent the intervening time fixing it up. Part of those preparations had included decorating a nursery, since she'd gotten pregnant only a few months after they were married. Still, they'd spent their entire wedded life together in that house, and the arrival of a little one was sure to change all the routines they'd grown used to.

"You just let me know when," I said. "And I'll be right there."

"That would be wonderful."

We chatted a little after that, but I could tell Stella was starting to get tired, easy delivery or no. I told the couple goodbye before heading out into the reception area. As I went I passed Tonya Willis, one of the witches in my mother's coven, and we nodded at each other, just as I'd nodded at Grace Bowersby a half hour earlier. It definitely looked to me as though everyone who could wanted to drop in and give Stella their best wishes.

I just hoped they wouldn't completely wear her

out, and that Kai would realize when it was time to say that visiting hours were over.

Right as I was fastening my seatbelt, my phone pinged.

Don't get your hopes up, I told myself as I pulled it out of my purse.

But that deprecating thought proved to be wrong, because the alert had signaled a text from Noah.

> Sorry I've been incommunicado. Things have been crazy. I have some good news, though. Tacos tomorrow night?

Since tomorrow was Tuesday, I couldn't think of anything better to have than tacos. And sure, maybe I would have liked to see Noah tonight, but I told myself that if things had been that busy at the clinic, he probably wanted the chance to just go home and crash.

> Sounds great. Your house or mine?

> My place @ 6:30?

> That works. See you then!

With that settled, I returned the phone to my

purse and finished fastening my seatbelt, smiling the whole time.

Noah hadn't been ignoring me. He was just swamped. And as for that good news?

Well, I supposed I'd find out tomorrow.

Chapter 12

Scot Free

"I'm going over to Noah's tonight," I told Cinny and Milo when I got home from work the next afternoon. "Is that okay with you?"

"Sure," Milo responded immediately, and Cinny gave a delicate flick of her tail.

"If I were by myself, I'm not sure I would like it," she told me. "But because I'll have Milo here, I think it will be fine."

My mouth quirked a bit at her solemn tone, but I tried to tamp down the smile, since I knew she was just trying to be truthful. "I won't be late," I promised. "So we'll still have time to watch TV together after I get home."

This plan seemed agreeable to both animals, and the three of us went into the yard to get some summer sunshine together before I headed inside to get tidied up a little for my evening at Noah's. I wasn't sure I could exactly call it a date, but at least we'd get to spend some time together after not seeing each other since Saturday night.

And I knew I'd be lying to myself if I didn't admit I was dying of curiosity as to what Noah's "news" would turn out to be.

After making sure both Cinny and Milo had fresh water in their bowls and their dinner dished out, I drove over to Noah's. It had been another beautiful day, warm but not hot, so I decided to roll down the windows and allow myself to breathe in the mild, sea-scented air.

Maybe the two of us could have our tacos *al fresco,* since I realized we hadn't spent any time in his backyard yet. I wondered a little at the omission, but thought it was possible we hadn't gone out there for the simple reason that he hadn't been able to get it fixed up yet.

When Noah opened his door in answer to my knock, he surprised me by giving me a quick kiss before I stepped inside.

"I missed you," he said.

I blinked. Oh, I'd missed him, too, but I honestly hadn't thought he'd make such an admission so early in our relationship. True, the guys I'd dated in the past had been a lot more closed off than Noah, so maybe I just wasn't used to being around someone who was okay with revealing what he was thinking.

"I missed you, too," I replied. After all, if he was going to be honest, then I needed to do him the courtesy of returning the favor. "But I figured you were swamped with work."

"That's for sure," he said. "I was hoping for a slowdown, but that hasn't happened yet. Anyway, I went ahead and ordered the food, since I remembered what you liked from Spitfire. I hope that's okay."

Under most circumstances, I wouldn't have been too thrilled to have a man ordering my meals for me. However, Spitfire Tacos didn't have the world's hugest menu, and because we'd gotten food there several times already, my preferences must have been pretty clear.

"No, that sounds great," I told him. "I'm hungry."

His expression cleared, and I could tell he'd been a little worried that I might take issue with the way he'd handled ordering our dinner. "Great. How about some wine while we wait for the food to show up?"

"Wine would be perfect."

We went into the kitchen, where a bottle of tempranillo was already sitting on the counter, along with a couple of stemless wine glasses. "If you want something white, I've got chardonnay in the fridge," Noah said.

Since I wasn't a huge fan of having white wine with food, I told him the tempranillo would be fine, and he uncorked the bottle and poured some for both of us. We'd both lifted our glasses to take a sip when the doorbell rang.

"Food's here," he said, somewhat unnecessarily. "Hang out here, and I'll go get it."

I waited in the kitchen but didn't drink any of my wine, thinking it would be kind of rude to start drinking while he was off dealing with the Door Dash driver. A moment later, Noah returned, a takeout bag in one hand.

"I was thinking we could eat outside, if that's okay," he suggested.

Was the guy psychic?

"That would be great," I replied. "I'll bring the wine."

So I picked up the bottle with my free hand, while he got his glass with the hand that wasn't holding the bag of takeout. We headed into the backyard, which was frankly kind of spectacular. True, it was smaller than my nearly an acre, but it had a lovely large deck with a seating area on one side and a table and four chairs on the other, while a fresh green lawn bordered by flowering plants took up the rest of the space.

"This is fabulous," I said as we sat down.

For some reason, he looked almost shamefaced. "Well, I can't take credit for any of it. The owner has been meaning to get the yard fixed up ever since I moved in, but after seeing how nice yours was, I pressured him a little, and he sent a bunch of people over to get all this installed."

Well, that answered my question about whether Noah owned his house or was just renting.

"The owner had this done in the past couple of days?" I asked, shocked that anyone could have pulled the backyard together so quickly. Now that I looked a little closer, I could tell the grass was sod that had just been laid, and there was some extra space between the plants in the border, giving them room to grow. Still, it all looked lovely.

Noah grinned as he started pulling tacos out of the bag. Because he'd set the table before I arrived, I already had a plate in front of me, so he could set my food directly on it. After he put his own tacos on his plate, he said, "Well, one of my clients at the clinic is a landscaper, and I'd given his info to my landlord. I guess Perry called him and asked if he'd be able to do the job in the next month so I'd still have time to enjoy it over the summer, and he told Perry he'd had a cancellation and could do it right now. So here we are."

A definite stroke of good luck. True, it wasn't a complicated garden design, nothing like my own expanse of herb gardens and flower borders and mature trees, but still, I was impressed that the landscaper had been able to pull it off in such a short amount of time...and impressed that Noah's landlord had been so conscientious about the whole thing.

Or maybe it wasn't really thoughtfulness at all, but something that had been written into the lease at signing and needed to be taken care of before it turned into a federal case.

"Here we are," I echoed, and raised my glass.

Noah clinked his against it, and we both drank some tempranillo, then went ahead and picked up the first of our tacos.

"So, that good news...?" I prompted.

"Right." He set down his taco and wiped his fingers on one of the paper napkins that had come with the food. "Shelby called me yesterday afternoon. She said the D.A. has decided to drop the charges."

For a second, I could only stare at Noah, startled by this turn of events. I'd thought the case was pretty flimsy, but I still hadn't imagined they'd dismiss the case against her this quickly. "What happened?"

"I guess the medical examiner went to the district attorney and told him that, based on the angle of the sword and how deep it went in, there was no way someone Shelby's height would have been able to strike that blow. The D.A. still wasn't too thrilled about the whole thing, but it sounds like he realized a jury would never believe she could have done such a thing, especially with all the physical evidence weighing against her being able to even commit that kind of crime."

Since I'd also thought pretty much the same thing—that Shelby wasn't physically capable of burying a sword in someone's back—this all made complete sense. I took a sip of tempranillo, then asked, "What happens now?"

"Well, Shelby's back in Boston, for one thing," Noah replied.

I did my best to maintain a straight face. Even though I knew Shelby Howard wasn't a threat to Noah's and my relationship, I couldn't help feeling much better now that I knew she was safely fifty miles away.

Obviously, I wasn't going to win any poker championships any time soon, because he chuckled and said, "Yeah, I kind of heaved a sigh of relief, too. I was doing my best to be supportive, but she and her mom can be kind of exhausting."

I couldn't really argue with that observation. At the same time, though, I wondered what Noah would think of my own mother. I loved her, but I also couldn't deny that she got on my nerves more often than I wanted to admit.

"And when were they going to tell me I was off the case?"

Another grin, this one even more dazzling because of the way the early evening sun flashed off his white teeth. "I suppose they were expecting me to pass the message along."

"So, that's why you wanted to see me?" I asked...not at all disingenuously.

Because he'd seen right through that question, Noah took another bite of his "vampiro" taco before replying. However, he still smiled a little as he said, "You know that's not the only reason."

No, it definitely wasn't. I suppose I'd thought that maybe a few days away from each other would do something about the way my knees seemed to go a little shaky every time he glinted those bright blue eyes of his at me. But no, sitting across the patio table from him, I knew absolutely nothing had changed about the way I felt about the man. If anything, the way he'd dominated my thoughts lately told me I was falling for this guy...and hard.

Exactly what I was supposed to do about that, I wasn't sure.

Since I didn't know how I should respond to his comment, I reached for my glass of wine and sipped from it. Noah's eyes twinkled at me, but he was silent as well, and had another bite of taco.

Once he'd washed down the morsel with some more wine, though, he said, "So...anything exciting happen over the past few days?"

"My friend Stella had her baby yesterday," I

blurted, since I knew I wasn't quite ready to confess that I'd gone to Boston on my day off to poke around at Miller & Miller.

"Stella from Tea & Sympathy?" he asked, surprising me.

"I didn't take you for the tea type," I said, and his mouth quirked a little.

"I'm not," he replied calmly. "But my mom is, and Stella's shop has some great gift baskets. I was in there a month or so ago getting something for my mother's birthday, and it was pretty obvious how pregnant Stella was."

Right. I had to remind myself that, even though Noah was a relative newcomer to Salem, he'd still been living here for more than a year and would have familiarized himself with a lot of the local shops and restaurants.

"She and her husband seem like a nice couple," he went on. "He's not from around here, is he?"

There was an understatement. Stella had met Kai in far northern Lapland, in frost elf country, when Jack Frost kidnapped Santa Claus and the couple had to effect a rescue or risk having Christmas never happen again. The frost elves had kept to themselves for millennia and had nothing to do with humankind, but Stella and Kai had fallen in love, and he'd moved to Salem to be with her.

"No," I replied, glad that my voice sounded

steady, "he's from Finland. They met when he was here on a tour."

Since that was the story they'd told everyone outside the witch community, I knew it wouldn't contradict whatever Noah might have heard previously...if anything. He definitely didn't seem like the gossipy type, and I doubted he would have had any reason to probe into Stella and Kai's background.

Noah tilted his head, as if to acknowledge my comment. Then he said, "Do you do much with them?"

Not as much as I should, I thought. I'd always been the kind of person to get caught up in day-to-day stuff, only to realize I hadn't connected with anyone outside work or caring for familiars for weeks at a time. That was probably part of the reason why Stella's and my friendship had waned over the past few years, although we seemed to have picked up where we'd left off without any acrimony over the gap in our socializing.

"When I can," I said, and added, "Although I think Stella and Kai are going to be pretty busy for the next couple of years."

Noah chuckled at that remark, as I'd hoped he would. Despite his good-humored response, I got the sense of a thousand unspoken words between us, as if we'd both been thinking about moving on to having a family, settling down, even though it was way too early in our relationship to be talking seriously about those subjects.

And I realized in that moment that I did want a future with him. What kind of future, I still wasn't exactly sure, but simply being with him was wonderful. Just listening to the sound of his voice, its warm timbre with just a touch of a Boston accent, or seeing the sun bring out flickers of gold and copper in his warm brown hair, made me happy in a way I knew I'd never been before.

Which might have been why I blurted, "I went to Miller & Miller yesterday."

Noah stared at me as if I'd just told him I'd taken a side trip to Zanzibar. "You what?"

I reached for my glass of wine, although I didn't immediately take a sip. Doing so would have only told him I was in need of liquid courage right then, and I didn't want to be quite that transparent.

"I guess I was feeling kind of stymied," I told him. "There didn't seem to be any clues here in Salem that would help me figure out who killed Trevor Miller, and I thought if I went and talked to one of his co-workers, got a clearer idea of who he really was, then maybe I'd have a better chance of learning the murderer's identity."

To my relief, Noah didn't appear upset by my confession. No, he still seemed more flummoxed than anything. "Were you actually able to talk to someone?"

"I was," I said, and recalled my promise to Bryce about not revealing who'd told me all those damning stories about Trevor. "One of the associates."

That seemed safe enough, since I'd read on the company's website that there were more than twenty of them. I doubted Noah would expend the effort to figure out which of those twenty people had spilled the beans to me.

"And?"

Although it felt kind of awful to speak so ill of someone so recently dead, I knew I needed to tell Noah what I'd learned during my foray to Boston. "They said that Trevor was actually an awful architect, and that everyone had to cover for him so he wouldn't make the company look bad."

That revelation made Noah's eyebrows go shooting up. "Seriously?"

"That's what they said. And then I asked if anyone at the firm harbored a big enough grudge against Trevor that they'd kill him over it, and the person I talked to said that didn't sound very likely. It's the kind of thing you might quit over, but not commit murder."

A long pause as Noah appeared to digest those revelations. Then he reached up to scratch the back of his head and said, "Maybe not...but it's something the police should look into."

"They already have," I told him. "At least, that's what the person I talked to said. It sounded more like the detectives wanted to know how the sword was stolen out of Trevor's office, but they also interviewed all the employees. From what I can tell, it doesn't seem as if the cops believed anyone at the firm was responsible."

Noah appeared to absorb all this, and asked, "So, they still don't have any idea how the sword was smuggled out of there?"

"It didn't sound like it," I said. "Which is kind of strange, because the building has security cameras everywhere. But that part is a total mystery right now."

And although I kind of wanted to avoid asking the question, I knew it wouldn't do any good to dance around the subject, not if we wanted to solve Trevor's murder.

"Do you think Shelby knew anything about Trevor? About what a crappy architect he was, I mean."

Noah was silent for a moment. "I don't know," he said. "She's always been the type of person who cares about appearances, so even if she'd known something, she would have kept it to herself." He hesitated there, as if trying to decide whether he should go any further, or whether he should leave the subject alone. Apparently, he decided he needed to keep going, because he added, "I think she was pretty invested in the idea of being married to the person who was going to inherit Miller & Miller, so she wouldn't have done anything to jeopardize that."

Probably not. And yet they'd apparently split up for a little while, or Shelby wouldn't have come here to Salem looking for Noah's shoulder to cry on. I was the kind of person who, once a relationship was over, didn't have anything to do with my ex after that, but obviously, Shelby didn't have a problem going to an ex-fiancé for emotional support if she thought he was the best person to ask for help.

And maybe she'd thought he was still harboring some guilt over their breakup, and had decided to exploit it.

All right, that wasn't a very charitable thought, and I knew I was maybe being a little hard on the woman.

"Did Shelby tell you why she and Trevor broke up?" I asked abruptly.

At once, Noah shook his head. "No. She said they had a disagreement but wouldn't say what it was about. I didn't want to be nosy, so I let it go."

Which didn't surprise me too much, since he'd made it pretty clear that he felt obligated to provide some emotional support but wasn't going to expend too much effort on analyzing the situation. And I couldn't blame him for feeling that way, because if one of my exes had appeared on my doorstep wanting me to hold their hand because of their relationship problems, I knew I would have shown them the door.

All the same, it seemed as if we were missing a piece of the puzzle here...and I could think of only one person who might be able to supply that missing piece.

"You said Shelby was back in Boston?" I asked.

"Yes—she and her mother left a couple of hours ago. Why?"

"Because I need to go there and ask her about her breakup with Trevor."

Chapter 13

Crazy Little Lies

Understandably, Noah didn't seem too thrilled by my plan. A slight frown pulling at his brow, he said, "I doubt Shelby's going to want to talk to you."

"Why not?" I countered. "Up until a few hours ago, she wanted me to solve the mystery. She might have had the murder charges dropped, but don't you think she's still going to want to know what really happened to Trevor?"

A long, uncomfortable pause, during which Noah rubbed his chin and looked as though he wished we were talking about almost anything else. "Maybe," he allowed at last, obviously not willing to commit to anything more than that.

"Well, that means it's worth a try," I said. "Obviously, it's too late now, but I can go tomorrow."

"Don't you have to work?"

"Yes," I said blithely, "but Sage can cover for me. It wouldn't be the first time."

With that particular objection shot down, Noah lapsed into silence for a moment. "All right," he said at last. "But you can't just show up. You need to at least ask if it's okay to go down there and talk to her."

"Fair enough," I responded. Personally, I thought it might have been a better idea not to give her any advance warning, but I saw where Noah was coming from. Shelby would know that I'd gotten her address from him, and might be justifiably pissed off if I showed up on her doorstep out of nowhere. I really didn't want to cause any trouble between the two of them, so I wasn't going to argue the point. "Can you give me her number?"

Although he didn't sigh, his expression was resigned as he dug his phone out of his jeans pocket. After he scrolled through his contacts list, he said, "It's 617-555-8722."

I'd also gotten out my phone, so it only took me a moment to enter her information. "Do you mind if I call now?"

"Go ahead," he said, sounding almost amused, as if he'd realized there wasn't anything he could do to stop me from going ahead with my plan, and he might as well sit back and wait for me to get the preliminaries over with.

And if Shelby shot me down, well, I'd figure out something else. But it seemed I needed to know the reason why she and Trevor had broken apart for a while when it seemed as though before that, she'd thought he was Mr. Perfect.

Her phone rang several times, and I crossed my fingers that it wouldn't go to voicemail. True, I'd called at a time when a lot of people were eating dinner—I'd definitely interrupted Noah's and my meal to make my call—so maybe she was ignoring her phone.

But then it picked up, and she said, "Hello."

She sounded brisk, almost cheerful, and not like someone who'd lost a fiancé to violence only a few days ago. I reminded myself that she'd been released from bail earlier today, and was quite possibly riding the high from that.

"Hi, Shelby, it's Charity."

"Charity?" she repeated, sounding surprised. Maybe she'd thought that now she'd been released, there was no reason for me to continue working on the case.

Before she could ask any awkward questions, I plowed forward. "It's great news that all the charges were dropped, but I'd still like to talk to you about a few things. Are you free tomorrow sometime?"

"Talk about what?" she asked, then went on

without waiting for a reply, "And we're talking now."

"I'd rather talk about it in person," I said. Maybe it was silly to insist on an in-person meeting, but you missed so much in a phone call. You couldn't see someone's expression, or be able to interpret their body language.

A second or two ticked by. Then she said, "I have a meeting with my lawyer in the morning, but I could meet you around two or three, if that's all right."

Even better. At least that way, I could put in a few hours at the shop before heading down to Boston. Since it was the middle of the week, I had to hope the traffic wouldn't be too bad.

"Then let's do two o'clock," I told her. Picking the earliest time Shelby would be home might have made me sound too eager, but honestly, I was just figuring the sooner I got there, the sooner I'd be able to leave and—with any luck—miss the worst part of the rush hour.

"Okay. My address is 52 Cambridge Street."

Even I knew that was in one of the most expensive neighborhoods in the city. Obviously, I didn't comment on that fact, only told Shelby I'd see her at two and then ended the call.

As I set down my phone, Noah was still wearing that half-amused expression. "You're like a dog with a bone."

"I don't like unanswered questions," I said. My mother would probably have pointed out that was part of me being a Virgo, that I liked everything neat and tidy, with no unfinished edges. I still wasn't sure how much I believed about astrology, but she'd gotten that part right.

"And you think this trip to talk to Shelby will give you those answers?"

I reached for my neglected taco and said, "I sure hope so."

* * *

After that, Noah and I both appeared to share an unspoken agreement that we needed to leave all talk of Shelby and Trevor's murder aside, and focused instead on our upcoming get-together with Jared and Kathy.

"Ah, that's the real reason why you pressured your landlord to get the backyard done," I joked, and Noah grinned in reply.

"You got me."

We talked about what we should barbecue, and whether I should make more of my potato salad or maybe branch out into some Boston baked beans.

"My mother has a great recipe for those," I said. "I'll get it from her."

And all right, I'd never made them before, but I

was sure if she coached me through the process, they should turn out just fine.

All during our conversation, the daylight had slowly faded. Before it became too dark, Noah went over to a switch that had been installed next to the French doors and flicked it on. At once, several strings of bistro lights came to life overhead.

I'd already thought the deck was fabulous, but lit up that way, it became absolutely magical. "Those are gorgeous!" I exclaimed.

"So are you," he replied as he came back over and then took my hands in his, helping me out of my chair.

It was probably too bright under those lights for him not to see my blush, but I tried to pretend it hadn't just happened. "Oh, I don't know about that," I said. Even though I knew it was silly to compare myself to her, I couldn't help contrasting my wild red hair with Shelby's smooth blonde locks, the way she seemed utterly put together no matter what catastrophes might be intruding in her life.

"Well, I do," Noah said, his tone firm. "When you walked into the clinic that first time last summer, it was all I could do to keep myself from staring."

"You could have fooled me," I joked. "You were completely professional."

"I didn't think flirting with one of my patients' owners was a very good look."

He wasn't exactly smiling, although his mouth was quirked at one corner. In that moment, he looked more delicious than ever.

"So...what made you change your mind?" I asked.

His fingers tightened on mine, and he pulled me a little closer, although he didn't bend down for a kiss. "It was easy to keep you at arm's length when you were coming into the clinic," he replied, his voice softer now, as caressing as the warm night-time breeze that tugged at my hair. "But when I saw you with Milo...when I saw how worried you were for him, even though he wasn't your own dog, I knew your heart was as beautiful as you are."

And then he did lower his head so he could press his lips against mine, and I tasted tempranillo and the faintest tang of chiles from our dinner on his mouth. Heat ran all through me, and I let myself fall into the embrace, forgetting Shelby and Trevor and the whole sad mess in that endlessly beautiful moment while we stood there in the illumination from the bistro lights strung overhead.

When he pulled away—not very much, only a couple of inches—he spoke again, this time in a husky whisper. "I'd love for you to come upstairs," he told me. "But if you're not ready, I understand."

My whole body told me I was ready. And

maybe it was crazy to do this the evening before I was going to meet his ex-fiancée, but on the other hand, I couldn't think of a better time. Shelby was his past.

And, incredible as it seemed to me even now, it appeared I was Noah's future.

Obviously, I couldn't stay the night, not with Milo and Cinny waiting for me at home. A little shamefaced, I thought of how I'd told them I wouldn't be out too late, and here it was almost ten o'clock.

"I need to get going," I whispered to Noah. "I've got the animals to check on."

He pushed a lock of coppery hair away from my face. The gesture was so gentle—and such a contrast to the passion he'd revealed just a short time earlier—that I almost lost my resolve. I wanted more than anything to stay here, to wake up in his arms and see how he liked to drink his coffee, whether he was the kind of guy who ate a real breakfast or whether he grabbed a granola bar on his way out the door.

Well, since it seemed like he wanted to keep me around, I had to hope I'd learn the answers to those questions sooner rather than later.

"It's fine," he said. "Maybe one time when

you're between fosters, you can bring Milo with you and stay the night."

"Or you could come over to my place," I replied. "I'll even make breakfast. Just don't expect French toast—I'm kind of an eggs and bacon kind of girl."

"Scrambled eggs?" he asked hopefully.

"Is there any other kind?" I joked.

We kissed again, and I did my best to ignore the reignited fire in my body so I could pull away from him, could pick up my clothes from where they lay strewn on the floor and get myself in some kind of reasonable shape.

"Dinner tomorrow night?" he asked as I zipped up my jeans. "I want to know how it went with Shelby."

I lifted an eyebrow. "Is that the only reason why you want to see me?"

"Come back to bed, and I'll show you how much I want to see you again," he suggested, the gleam in his eyes apparent even in the darkened room, lit only by the ceiling fixture in the upstairs hallway.

I chuckled. "I wish. But I really do need to get home."

He didn't argue, but instead reached for his underwear and jeans and pulled them on. Then he walked me down to the front door, and gave me a goodnight kiss. Not an entirely chaste one, but I could tell he was holding back, not wanting to get either of our motors running when he knew I had obligations back at my house.

"Pick you up at seven," he said, and I nodded.

"Sounds perfect."

Then I hurried down the front steps and got into my Land Rover. It wasn't so late that Noah and I couldn't have been doing something perfectly innocent, like sitting on his deck and talking, or hanging out in his living room and watching TV. Even so, going to my vehicle felt like a definite walk of shame, as though the entire neighborhood had already guessed exactly what we'd been up to.

I drove sedately, even though I knew the wine we'd had with dinner had completely burned off. It just seemed safer that way, since I didn't really want to get pulled over with my hair mussed and my makeup completely worn off...and, no doubt, a few telltale marks on my throat.

Milo and Cinny were sleeping in the living room when I got home, but they perked up as soon as I walked in. The dog tilted his head just the littlest bit, as if he could tell I'd come home much later than promised.

"Sorry," I said, hoping I sounded blithe and unconcerned, and not as though Noah Jenkins hadn't completely rocked my universe less than an hour earlier. "I guess the time got away from me."

A sniff, and then a knowing light gleamed in Milo's eyes.

Oh, dear lord. He must have been able to smell exactly what I'd been up to.

But since I wasn't about to discuss my sex life with a dog, even one as smart and wonderful as Milo, I did my best to breeze past the moment. "Do you need to go out?"

Kind of a silly question, because my kitchen had a dog door, and he could come and go as he pleased. But there was something different about being let out, and he nodded and said, "Yes, please."

Cinny really didn't need to go outside at all, since her litter box had taken up temporary residence in my laundry room. However, she followed Milo outside anyway, maybe so she could smell the night air and get a sense of the lay of the land before she went to bed.

Or—and I thought this was a distinct possibility—she had such a case of hero worship that she didn't want to let him out of her sight.

They didn't spend too much time outside, though, and we were all tucked away in bed well before eleven.

It was hard to fall asleep, though. I kept thinking of Noah's touch, of how it had felt to be in his arms, and wondered if he was lying wakeful in the bed I'd occupied only an hour or so earlier. I thought of the quantum leap we'd just taken, and what would come next.

If we stayed together...if this got as serious as I thought it might...then sooner or later, I'd have to tell him the truth about me. I didn't want to, though. Not just because of the risk involved, but because I didn't want him to look at me any differently. I'd seen the way he gazed into my eyes earlier this evening, like I was some kind of goddess descended to Earth to consort with a mere mortal.

I wasn't a goddess, though.

I was only a woman.

And a witch. Whether Noah would be able to deal with that uncomfortable reality was a question I preferred to put off for as long as possible.

Luckily, there weren't so many telltales from the hours I'd spent with Noah that I couldn't easily cover them up with concealer. Most days, I didn't wear a lot of makeup, but I took my time with it this morning, telling myself I needed to look as polished as possible for my meeting with Shelby.

Right.

I didn't tell the animals I was going to Boston, mostly because I hoped to be back before I was expected home, somewhere between five-thirty and six. They were used to me disappearing for most of the day, since I usually didn't have enough time to come home for lunch.

However, I gave Cinny a salmon treat after her breakfast and asked, "How are you doing?"

"Better," she said after a thoughtful pause. "Being here has helped, I think. I'm still sad that I won't get to have my kittens, but Milo has helped me understand that it's a very important thing to be a familiar, that we provide something for our mistresses that no one else can. Now I can look at the situation a little differently."

I reflected that Milo was doing a better job of being a familiar-whisperer than I was. Then again, he wasn't trying to solve a murder at the same time.

Right before I left, I scratched him behind the ears and told him he was a good boy, and I'd have to figure out a way to reward him for the way he'd helped me with Cinny.

His tail wagged, but he only said, "I'm glad I could be here for her. I don't need a reward."

"Well, I'll still come up with something," I promised, then hurried out the door.

After all, I didn't want to be late when I knew I'd have to ask Sage to watch the shop on her own this afternoon.

But when I told her I needed to go to Boston that afternoon, she didn't seem too worried.

"You gotta do what you gotta do, right?" she told me, and I had to agree.

I only hoped it would be worth taking the time off.

It also seemed as if I'd done a pretty good job of appearing sunny and casual and as though my entire life hadn't changed the night before, because Sage didn't seem to notice anything different about me. Or maybe she did, but had realized it probably wasn't a good idea to bring up such a personal subject with her boss. In general, our relationship was more one of friends than supervisor and employee, but at bottom, she still worked for me, and probably understood there were some lines you shouldn't cross.

Maybe it was because of what happened last night that I was a bit more tense driving south than I probably should have been. I told myself over and over again that Shelby didn't know me well enough to be able to sense any kind of difference...but what if she did?

Well, as my mother liked to say, I'd cross that bridge after I burned it.

The traffic wasn't bad, at least, and I made good time. In fact, I was a few minutes early, and rather than park in front of Shelby's house and wait there like a stalker or something, I drove around the neighborhood a bit, taking in the huge, stately homes, many of which looked as though they'd been there from the time of the Revolutionary War, and tried to rehearse how I'd ask that crucial question about Trevor without sounding like an utter witch.

Pardon the phrase.

But no matter how I went about it, the truth was ugly enough that I knew the words were going to sound terrible despite my best efforts. About all I could do was hope that Shelby already knew the reality of the situation, and at least what I was about to tell her wouldn't come as a complete surprise.

My wandering burned up enough time that I was able to circle back and park in front of Shelby's house a few minutes after two. I had to admit that my fifteen-year-old Land Rover Discovery looked very out of place in the upscale neighborhood, and even though I generally didn't care how fancy a vehicle was as long as it got me from Point A to Point B, I still found myself wishing I'd stopped to get the SUV washed before coming down here.

Or maybe I was just worrying about minor stuff like that because it was easier than trying to guess how this interview was going to go.

I was here now, though, and that meant the only thing I could do was get out of the damn car, walk up the brick walkway between two equally manicured green lawns—the kind of grass I wouldn't be surprised was measured with a ruler to make sure it was a uniform length— and get this over with.

The place was so fancy that I was kind of surprised to see Shelby herself answer the doorbell, rather than a butler or a housekeeper or something. She was wearing a cream linen sheath dress that I knew would have been a wrinkled mess if it had been on my own body, and her blonde hair was pulled back into a simple, elegant ponytail.

"Come inside," she told me, stepping out of the way so I could move into the foyer.

It was as perfect as the exterior of the house, with a black and white checkerboard floor of imported marble and a vase of creamy green-white hydrangeas on a round table in the center of the space.

"We can talk in here," she went on, guiding me into a sitting room just off the entryway. "Would you like anything to drink? Tea? Lemonade? Water?"

I was pretty thirsty...nerves, no doubt.

"Water would be fine," I replied, since my nerves were shot enough without throwing any caffeine or sugar into the mix.

"Go ahead and sit down," she said, gesturing toward a prim little settee upholstered in pale blue silk. "I'll be right back."

The settee didn't look very comfortable, but I knew I needed to take a seat. I sat down and sent a quick glance around me, taking in the perfectly matched parlor palms that flanked a carved console table on one side, the somehow forbidding land-scapes that decorated the walls.

It definitely didn't look like the sort of house that would be occupied by a vibrant woman in her early thirties. Maybe she'd inherited the place, or maybe she'd decorated it this way because that was what was expected of the scion of an old Boston family.

Shelby returned with a silver tray that bore a pair of crystal water glasses and a pitcher to match. Waterford, I guessed, since I doubted this house contained anything that had been bought at Target or HomeGoods.

She set the tray down on the Hepplewhite coffee table, then sat on one of the delicate chairs, upholstered in the same blue silk, that faced the settee. After we'd both picked up our glasses, she said, "So, what was so important that you couldn't talk to me on the phone? Do you have a lead about who killed Trevor?"

"No," I replied, then added hastily as her smooth forehead began to pucker, "not yet, anyway." I pulled in a breath and told myself I needed to pull on my big-witch panties. "But this is about Trevor."

Shelby's gaze flicked toward a tall window with fanlight detailing that overlooked the property's front lawn. The street seemed utterly quiet and the house appeared to be empty, and yet I couldn't quite shake the feeling that she was worried about someone overhearing us.

"What about Trevor?"

Her voice was level enough, but I thought I saw her mouth tighten almost imperceptibly as she spoke his name.

"What caused your split? What made you come up to Salem?"

One perfectly groomed eyebrow lifted slightly. "Those are awfully personal questions."

"I know," I said. "But there had to have been some reason." I stopped there, steeling myself. No, I shouldn't just blurt it out, but I also couldn't sidestep the issue. "Was it because of the way he'd had his associates covering for him so no one would find out what a bad architect he really was?"

Shelby's head went up then, and she stared at me in shock. With a shaking hand, she set down her glass of water, still untouched. "How did you know about that?"

Well, at least Trevor's complete failure in that area wasn't a surprise to his fiancée. "Someone at the firm told me," I said, and quickly added, "And no, I'm not going to say who. They spoke in confidence, and I'm going to respect that, because it would probably be their job on the line if Mr. Miller or someone else high up at the firm found out who it was."

An uncomfortable pause. Shelby's eyes had

narrowed slightly, and I could almost see her doing the mental calculations, trying to decide whether there was some way she could cajole or bully me into revealing my source. She must have decided that wasn't going to work, though, most likely because she didn't have any real leverage over me. I wasn't her employee, and Noah had already made it pretty clear where his loyalties lay.

"That's what we fought about," she said at last. "He told me he was tired of living a lie, and wanted to come clean about his situation and quit."

"And you weren't on board with that plan?"

She rubbed a hand against the pale linen of her skirt. It seemed she didn't have sweaty palms, though, because she didn't leave a mark behind.

"Of course not," she replied, her tone seeming to indicate she thought I was an idiot for believing otherwise. "It wasn't even about the money—Trevor has a trust from his grandfather. No, I just didn't want to be married to a laughingstock."

That's some real emotional support there, I thought. However, Noah's description of his split from Shelby had already told me she seemed to be a "my way or the highway" kind of person, so I supposed I shouldn't be too surprised that she wanted Trevor to continue with his charade so she could be married to a man everyone thought was a true success.

"I'm sure he took that really well," I said dryly, and she sent me a withering look.

"You've never moved in our circles, so of course you wouldn't understand. What difference did it make if his associates did all the work?"

"You mean besides lying about the whole thing and making your fiancé feel like a total fraud?" I returned.

Eyes still narrowed, she said, "It wasn't a big deal. But he didn't see it that way, said he was going to speak with his father and tell him he was leaving the family business. He was even going to go into work and apologize to his associates for the way he'd been using them ever since he came to work for the firm after college."

Wow. I couldn't help being impressed by that revelation. It would have been one thing to slip away quietly, to cook up some story about illness or needing a change of scenery or whatever, but to stand up in front of the people you'd been exploiting for years and say you were sorry for your behavior?

That was the mark of someone who deserved a much better fate than what he'd received.

"But you weren't thrilled with that plan," I remarked.

Shelby reached for her glass of water, took one deliberate swallow, and then set it back down on the tray. "Of course I wasn't. I told Trevor if he was going to do that, then we were through. He pleaded with me, but I said I needed to leave, that I needed to go someplace where I could think everything over." Her eyes met mine, not narrowed now, but almost opaque, as though she was doing her best to ensure I couldn't get a glimpse of what was going on in her mind. "And that's when I came up to Salem. Noah was always a good person to talk things over with, and that's why I went to his place to see him."

Yes, I had to agree that Noah was easy to talk to. That didn't mean I was happy about his ex-fiancée using him as a sounding board.

Especially when she'd introduced herself to me as his current fiancée.

I almost asked why she'd done such a crappy thing, then decided it really didn't matter. Noah was clearly over Shelby, and was all too ready to leave her in his rearview mirror.

"Do you know if Trevor actually talked to his father?"

Her shoulders lifted, tanned against the creamy linen of her sleeveless dress. Was the tan natural, or did she go to a salon?

Not that it really mattered.

"He didn't say," she said after a pause. "He came up to Salem and was full of apologies, brought me a diamond bracelet, said things were going to be different. I asked him what he meant by that, and all he said was that he'd done what he had to do and was going to make sure he gave me the happiest life possible."

Promises I assumed Shelby had taken at face value, since she'd already told Noah and me that the two of them had gone out to eat not too long after he met her at the cottage. "And you took him back."

"Yes," she replied. "He seemed so cheerful and upbeat, like a huge weight had lifted off his shoulders. I had to believe that meant he'd made his peace with the situation and was going to do whatever he could to make sure we had a good future together. And then...."

The words trailed off, but she didn't have to finish the sentence. We both knew that happy future had never materialized, that when he'd uttered those words, Trevor could have had no idea he was only going to live for a few more hours.

"I'm so sorry," I said, and hoped she could hear the sincerity in my voice.

It looked like she had, because her expression was sad but also resigned, as though she'd gotten to a place where she could, if not exactly accept what had happened, at least try to look forward and decide what she wanted to do next.

"Why are you still trying to figure out what happened?" she asked next. "I mean, I know I asked you to help, but now that the charges have been dropped...."

"I like closure," I said, which seemed like the simplest explanation. Because Lorna and Thad Miller had come to me in confidence, I couldn't tell Shelby that Trevor's parents also had a vested interest in knowing the truth, and that I hoped to discover it sooner rather than later so they could have some closure as well.

To my relief, it looked as though Shelby had taken my words at face value, because she only nodded. "Is there anything else?"

Not that I could think of, and I'd probably brought up a lot of pain she'd been doing her best to bury. Everyone handled their grief differently, but I got the feeling Shelby Howard was the sort of person who wanted to put things behind her as quickly as possible and get on with her life.

"No, that was it," I replied. "Thanks for talking with me."

She gave a small lift of her shoulders, then rose from her chair. I got up, too, and let her walk me to the door. As she opened it, she said, "This thing with you and Noah."

I swallowed, and did my best to maintain a neutral expression. Had she somehow guessed we'd taken the next step in our relationship only the night before?

"Yes?" I said.

"It's serious, isn't it." The words came out flat—a statement, not a question.

"Um...maybe."

Maybe one eyebrow lifted slightly. However, all she said was, "Good to know."

And she opened the door and I hurried out, wondering why she'd asked the question. Had she secretly hoped she still might be able to get back with Noah?

Possibly. But the resigned expression she'd worn as I turned away from her to walk down the front steps told me she knew that was never going to happen.

Thank God.

Chapter 14

Mama's House

The whole way back to Salem, I kept brooding over my conversation with Shelby, picking it apart, trying to see if there was some nuance I'd missed, something she'd said that didn't ring true.

But no matter how hard I tried, I couldn't come up with anything that seemed to fit. I had to admit she appeared remarkably composed for a woman who'd lost her fiancé only a few days earlier, but some people weren't given to showy displays of emotion...or maybe it was more that she refused to indulge in them around me.

It was a little after four when I got into town, and while I supposed I could have headed over to the store and helped Sage until closing time swung around at five, there didn't seem to be much point.

Having me there for less than an hour wouldn't help very much.

Instead, I made a mental note to give her a raise. We were coming up on her one-year anniversary at the store in a few months anyway.

Milo and Cinny were sunning themselves in the yard when I got home, which seemed like a very good use of their time, considering it was another picture-perfect day.

"I can tell you missed me," I said with a grin.

The dog didn't even bother to appear offended. "It would have been better to have you home," he replied. "But since you weren't, we decided to enjoy ourselves out here."

Fair enough. Because I'd been running around so much this week, I realized our stock on a few items we needed at the store was getting pretty low, and since Noah wouldn't be picking me up until seven, I knew I had some time to throw a couple of tinctures together.

"I'm going to work in the kitchen for a little while," I told the familiars. "But feel free to stay out here for as long as you like."

"Kitchen?" Cinny repeated hopefully. For a cat, she sure did love table scraps.

"Just making a few potions," I told her, and tried not to smile at the deflated expression she immediately assumed.

But since I wasn't cooking up anything interesting, both animals seemed happy to remain in the yard. I went inside and got out the iron cauldron I used to make my tinctures and elixirs, and poured some spring water into it, then got busy collecting the herbs and other ingredients I needed for my insomnia potion, which was by far the most popular item at Full Moon Apothecary.

Within a half hour, it was simmering away on the stovetop, sending scents of chamomile and valerian and a dash of hops into the air. Focusing on adding all the ingredients in the proper order and chanting a sleep spell over them helped to distract me from the conundrum of Trevor's murder, and did a good job of bringing my jangly energy levels down to something a bit more manageable.

But just as I was about to turn down the flame on the stove so the elixir could begin to cool, my phone rang.

The number didn't look familiar, but I went ahead and picked up anyway. "This is Charity."

A woman's voice, cool, almost familiar. "Hello, Charity. This is Lorna Miller."

"Oh, hi," I replied, even as a pang of guilt went through me. Had she somehow figured out that I'd gone to visit Shelby Howard?

Not that there was really anything to be guilty about, except that Shelby was privy to a few secrets Lorna might not have wanted me to know.

"I don't suppose you have any news for us," Lorna said.

"No, I don't," I replied. "There really isn't much evidence to work with."

"Apparently," she said, her tone crisp. "Well, then, I suppose it's a good thing that Trevor's father and I have retained the services of a private detective, so we won't need you to keep looking into the case."

That announcement had come from out of left field. True, a few days had passed since the Millers had come into the shop to talk to me, but I'd just sort of assumed they were going to give me more time than that to see if I could dig up any concrete evidence.

However, I was just fine with being fired. I wasn't a professional, so it was much better that she and her husband had hired one to take over the case.

"I totally understand," I said. "I'm sorry I couldn't come up with anything for you."

"It's fine," she replied, in tones that seemed to indicate she thought it was definitely anything but fine. "We just wanted to let you know. Have a good afternoon."

And she ended the call there, while I held my phone for a moment and wondered if there was something else I was missing here. Lorna's tone had been brisk and no-nonsense, but a certain tension had underlaid it, as if she wasn't entirely happy about giving me the boot.

Had her husband given her some marching orders?

I'd barely put my phone down on the kitchen table before it rang again.

Noah's number.

The iPhone was back in my hand in a flash. "Hi, Noah," I said. "What's up?"

"I'm having kind of an emergency here," he replied. "Someone brought in a street cat who was hit by a car, but I wasn't able to save her. She had a litter of kittens."

"Oh, no," I said. "How many kittens?"

"Four. They look like they're about a week old, definitely not old enough to be weaned. My assistants are feeding them with bottles right now—thank God the kittens are old enough for that—but we're searching for someone who can foster them until they're old enough to be adopted."

Foster them....

A crazy idea popped into my head, one I wanted to brush off as being completely improbable.

Then again, what was magic for if not to achieve the impossible?

"Bring them over here," I said. "Cinny can take care of them."

A long pause. I couldn't see Noah's face, but I

had to believe he was looking incredulous right then. "Charity," he said, his patient tone indicating that he wanted to let me down gently, "Cinnamon's a great cat, and I'm sure she'd be good with the kittens, but she won't be able to nurse them. You'd have to feed them with a bottle for weeks."

"It's fine," I said cheerfully. "I can be as flexible with my work hours as I need to be, and that means I'd be here for the kittens. You know I love animals, and I've worked with all kinds. It'll be fine."

"You're sure?" he asked. Now he sounded as though he wanted to be hopeful but wasn't certain whether or not he could allow himself to.

"Absolutely. Can you bring the kittens over after you're done at the clinic for the day?"

"Sure," Noah said. "My last appointment is at a quarter to five, so I can probably be at your house around five-thirty."

That gave me about an hour. It should be enough...I hoped.

"See you then," I told him.

Voice still a little dazed, he echoed, "See you then."

I went over to the stove and turned off the flame beneath the cauldron. Luckily, I knew that extra ten minutes or so of heat wouldn't have hurt anything, and because I had to allow the elixir to cool all the way before I could start bottling it, I had hours and hours before I needed to touch it again.

That task handled, I headed outside to the yard and grinned down at Cinnamon, who was lying on her side, soaking up the sun. Good thing she'd had such a relaxing couple of days, because things were about to get a lot more hectic for her.

"Hey, Cinny," I said. "Ready to be a momma?"

* * *

I had plenty of cauldrons of various sizes tucked away in my kitchen, so I selected a small one to create the potion that would allow Cinnamon to nurse the kittens Noah was bringing over. Before I sent her home to Doris, I'd have to make up enough to ensure she would be able to keep suckling her newly acquired family until they were ready to be weaned, but before I brewed up a huge batch, I needed to make sure the elixir I'd visualized would do its job.

The cat was practically bouncing with excitement, watching as I dropped powdered milk thistle and dandelion root and burdock into the cauldron, sniffing the air as the ingredients eventually congealed into a thick white substance that looked more like heavy cream than anything else.

"That's really going to give me milk?" she asked.

"That's the plan," I responded cheerfully. "We just need to wait a few minutes for this to cool down, and then you can have some before Noah comes over."

"When's he going to get here?"

I glanced at the clock on the stove. "In about twenty minutes or so."

Cinny rolled her green eyes, as if twenty minutes sounded as though it was a lifetime from now. For myself, I was glad we had that much time left.

We were going to need all of it.

And yes, I knew I probably should have called Doris to let her know her familiar might be going home with a litter of kittens, but I didn't see the point in getting her riled up until I knew for sure that the potion was going to work.

A few anxious moments passed while we all waited for the milky liquid to cool down. Milo was a little more used to my potion-making—although he'd never seen me attempt anything like this before—but he still looked on with interest, obviously curious to see whether I'd be able to pull off this particular feat.

Then I got out a dropper, filled it with the potion, and went over to Cinny, who'd been watching me with eagle eyes the entire time. "I can't vouch for the taste," I told her. "But you need to take all of it."

"Not a problem," she declared, and opened her pink mouth, showing needle-sharp little teeth.

At least with a familiar, I didn't have to worry about those teeth getting buried in the fleshy part of my hand if she decided she didn't like the taste after all. I squeezed all the contents of the dropper into her mouth, and she obediently swallowed them without a single complaint, although her nose wrinkled slightly.

"Now what?" she asked. "I don't feel any different."

"You're sure?"

A tilt of her head, and then she brushed an orange paw across her stomach. As the thick fur parted, I could see that all her nipples had gotten bigger. And was that a drop of milk emerging from one of them?

"It worked!" she exclaimed.

That it had. Or at least, it looked as though Cinny was producing milk.

The trick now was seeing whether the kittens would drink it.

However, the cat didn't appear too worried, because she went over to the bed I'd set up in a corner of the kitchen, prepped with soft little blankets for the arrival of the kittens, and curled up in it, obviously ready to get to work as soon as the orphans arrived.

Which wasn't too much longer, because Noah

knocked at the door about five minutes later, a box of kittens in his arms and a worried expression on his face.

"You're sure about this?" he asked, and I nodded.

"Absolutely. Come on in."

I led him through the living room and into the kitchen, then pointed toward the spot where Cinny lay in her bed. The cat looked up as soon as we entered the space, but it appeared as though she knew she needed to remain where she was and have the kittens brought to her.

Noah, however, seemed dubious. "It's great that your cat wants to cuddle with the kittens," he said. "But someone else is going to have to feed them."

"Maybe," I allowed. "Just take the kittens to her."

Still wearing that skeptical expression, he walked over to Cinny's bed, put the box of kittens on the floor, and then carefully began to pick them up and set them in the bed with her. They were all making little meeping noises, obviously worried about being in a strange new place, but as soon as Cinny moved closer and they smelled her milk, they immediately latched on and started nursing.

Noah straightened, staring down at the new family in amazement. "Wait...how is that even possible? She's sterile!"

"I know," I said calmly. "I fixed up a little folk remedy for her."

"'A folk remedy,'" he repeated, arms crossed as he stared down at the kittens—two of them ginger like Cinny, one a gray tabby, the other a calico—who were attached to Cinnamon's belly, all of them oblivious to anything else happening in their surroundings.

Honestly, my claim that I'd used a folk remedy wasn't even a lie. A lot of my potions were based on old, old concoctions that had been used for centuries. True, I sprinkled some magic into them to make sure they were far more potent and effective, but the original recipe I'd based Cinny's milk-producing potion on had been originally invented for much the same reason, for women whose milk hadn't started, for whatever reason.

"That's the kind of stuff I sell in my shop, you know," I pointed out.

Noah looked away from the cat and her newfound family, and sent me a rueful smile. "You sell lactating formulas for cats?"

Since he seemed more befuddled than anything else, I couldn't take offense at his wry tone. "Well, not those exactly, but I make all sorts of tinctures and tonics and elixirs for a variety of problems. And they work. So it wasn't that hard to go through my books and make something custom for Cinny."

"It's still pretty remarkable."

Because agreeing with him would have made me sound like I had a swelled head, I settled for a small lift of my shoulders. "To be honest, I wasn't really sure whether it would work or not. But I figured it would be worth a try. Cinny wanted a family, and even if the elixir didn't do what I wanted it to do, she could at least give them some comfort while I took care of bottle feeding them."

"'Cinny wanted a family'?" Noah repeated. "How did you know that?"

Oops. I'd been so caught up in the moment, I'd kind of forgotten that there was no real way I could have known about the cat's desire for a family if I was just a regular woman who didn't have any witchy powers.

"Oh, that's part of why I was watching her," I said quickly. "Her owner swore up and down that Cinny was pining for kittens, so I said I'd take her for a week and see if I could get to the bottom of it."

"And how did her owner know she wanted kittens?"

Make this good, I told myself. "Because whenever Cinny would see kittens on TV—you know, in a commercial or a show—she'd go up to the screen and try to touch it, like she wanted to see if they were real. And when a neighbor's cat had kittens, Cinny ran out the door as soon as Doris opened it and headed straight over there. She tried to cuddle with them, but the mama cat had other ideas."

"I can see how she might," Noah responded, his tone dry.

But because he hadn't tried to poke any holes in my story, I told myself he must have bought it, or at least had decided it was plausible enough that he wasn't going to ask any more questions.

"So, when I heard about the kittens you rescued, I thought I might as well see if the elixir would work on her," I went on. "Someone I know who's a lactation expert has used it on some of her clients, and since it helped them, I thought it might help Cinny. It doesn't have any ingredients that would harm a cat, so I figured the worst that would happen was that it wouldn't do anything at all."

Again, not really a lie. A witch over in Marble-head actually was a lactation coach, and when she told me about some of the issues her clients were having, I'd put together a batch of the potion to see if it would do anything. It had turned out to be such a success that I continued to make the elixir for her, although I didn't carry it in my shop because it was kind of a specialty item.

"Well, it definitely did something," Noah remarked. He looked back over at the kittens. Two of them—the calico and the gray-striped one—seemed to have already drunk their fill, since they'd stopped nursing and were now curled up against Cinny, their tiny eyes shut tight. The two orange ones were still going at it, but I had to believe they'd be sated soon enough as well. Mouth turning up at one corner, he added, "I have a feeling we're not going out to dinner tonight."

Oh, right. We'd had dinner plans, but the arrival of the kittens had pretty much torpedoed that idea. "We can get takeout," I suggested.

"Probably a good idea," Noah said, and at once Milo's ears perked up. Yes, he was okay with me going out with Noah because he approved of the man, but much better for us to eat here so he could beg some table scraps off us.

That was why we got Door Dash to bring us some Thai, and why we took it out to the garden so we could eat at the table there and enjoy the last of the warm day. Obviously, Cinny couldn't accompany us, but the tilt of her head I'd glimpsed as Noah headed outside with the takeout bags and Milo and I tagged along told me she was just fine with staying where she was.

Noah and I sat at the table while the dog curled up nearby, ready to go if someone should offer him a morsel of chicken or shrimp. Yes, I'd dutifully filled his bowl, but I knew he wasn't going to eat any of his kibble until he'd made sure we were done with our own meal.

"So," Noah said, once we'd dished up our food

and poured some wine. I didn't have any rosé, which was what I really liked with Asian food, but a crisp Italian white worked well enough. "What happened with your trip to Boston?"

I'd kind of hoped all the excitement with Cinny and the kittens had made him conveniently forget about my visit with Shelby, but obviously, it was still occupying his mind.

"She knew," I said briefly, and speared a piece of cashew chicken with my fork.

"That Trevor was a fraud?" Noah replied, expression startled.

I nodded, ate the piece of chicken, and said, "I guess he confessed to her. Honestly, it kind of sounded to me like she was on board with him continuing to lie if it meant nothing would change about his position at the firm. He didn't seem too cool with that, although Shelby didn't give me any specifics about what he planned to do next. He just told her that he had it figured out and that he was going to make sure they had a great life together."

"And that's why she took him back?"

"It seems that way. Maybe he planned to tell her more, but he was killed before he could say anything else."

"Damn." Noah set down his fork so he could reach for his wine and take a sip.

That seemed like a good idea, so I picked up my own glass and had a swallow. It was one thing to talk coolly and calmly about the hows and whys behind Trevor's murder, but I could never let myself forget that a man had been brutally killed. "Anyway," I went on, "nothing she said gave me the slightest clue as to who might have wanted to kill him. I mean, I'm glad she was honest with me about what Trevor said to her, but since it didn't really clear anything up, I'm not sure it was worth going down there to talk to her."

"Maybe not," Noah responded. "Or maybe something she said will make more sense later. At least you tried."

I had...to no avail, as far as I was concerned. True, Shelby was off the hook legally, and it seemed the Millers didn't have any use for my services, either, so I knew I should probably let the whole thing go and get on with my life.

On the other hand, I really didn't like unanswered questions. Who had entered the cottage that night and murdered Trevor with his own sword? Maybe even more importantly, *why* had they done such a thing? And why a sword, of all things? Wouldn't it have been easier to have bought a gun on the black market and handle the situation that way?

"Do you think it's possible one of Trevor's clients found out he was a fraud and killed him over it?" Noah asked next.

That scenario sounded remotely probable, but....

"Isn't that the kind of thing you usually settle with a lawsuit and not a sword in someone's back?"

Noah chuckled, although there was a grim note to the sound, as if he'd realized this whole thing really wasn't a laughing matter. "You're probably right about that. Well, I guess we'll just have to hope the Salem police will figure it out eventually."

Since there didn't seem to be anything else either of us could do, I found myself in reluctant agreement. I made a noncommittal sound, and Noah seemed to understand I wanted to move on from that particular subject. We talked about the barbecue coming up at his place on Saturday night, and about Cinnamon and her new family.

"I really need to call Doris after we're done eating," I said. "She's supposed to pick up Cinny tomorrow morning, and I don't want to spring the whole thing about the kittens on her right when she shows up."

"Yeah, I'd say it's definitely better to let her know in advance," he agreed. "What're you going to do if she freaks out about it?"

"Keep Cinny here until the kittens are old enough to be adopted," I said promptly. While I thought that was a remote possibility, I knew I had to plan for the contingency, just in case. Because Cinnamon was obviously capable of taking care of the kittens—provided I kept mixing up batches of the lactation potion for her—I didn't think it would be too much trouble to keep her for the next couple of months.

Somehow, though, I doubted Doris would want to be without her familiar for such a long stretch of time.

Which proved to be the case when I called her a little after that. Noah had offered to take care of the meal's minimal clean-up...basically, putting our plates and utensils in the dishwasher...so I took my phone out to the living room, glad to have a little privacy to make the call.

After I explained the situation, there was a dumbfounded silence on Doris's end. I looked down at my phone, but no, we were still connected.

"She has kittens," Doris said at last, her tone flat.

"Well, she's adopted them, but yes," I replied. "I know I should have called you first, but it all happened so fast...."

I let the words trail off into the ether and hoped she would understand that there hadn't been a lot of thinking involved, just pure reaction.

After an uncomfortable silence, she said, "It is what it is, I suppose. I certainly wouldn't want those poor kittens to be left out on the street, and Cinny has been pining for a family. If I believed in such things, I'd say it was providence. Anyway, you can expect me at ten tomorrow morning, just like we planned. It looks like tonight I'll have to make some arrangements to have a bunch of kittens here."

"Oh, they really won't be that much work—" I began, only to have Doris cut me off, her tone crisp.

"We had cats when I was a little girl, before Cinnamon came into my life. Believe me, I know exactly how much work kittens can be. See you tomorrow."

She ended the call there, just as Noah came into the room. He sent me an inquisitive glance, and I mustered a smile.

"All taken care of," I told him. "Doris is on board with the kittens, and will pick up the whole family tomorrow morning. It sounds like she's dealt with cat families before, so I think they'll be in good hands."

"Good to hear." He came closer, and pushed my hair aside so he could place a kiss on the back of my neck. A delicious little thrill went through me, and even though a moment earlier I would have said I definitely wasn't in the mood for anything except maybe putting my feet up and watching some TV, I thought there were probably a few other things he and I could do together that would be a much better use of our time.

Besides, Cinny was in the kitchen with the

kittens, and Milo had stayed there with them, as though he thought they needed some kind of bodyguard.

"Let's go upstairs," I murmured.

"Thought you'd never ask."

And later, as I lay in Noah's arms and listened to him breathe deeply...knowing that I'd need to wake him up soon, since he hadn't even brought a toothbrush with him...I thought that things had ended pretty well for Cinny.

If only I could say the same thing for poor Trevor Miller.

Chapter 15

Wild Cards

Noah left around ten-thirty, and after checking on Cinny—she was fast asleep, with all the kittens snuggled up next to her and Milo lying a few paces away—I climbed the stairs and began getting ready for bed. It was strange to think of being up here by myself, since the dog had been a constant companion while I slumbered ever since he'd become a part of my life, but I knew he thought his first responsibility was to Cinnamon and the kittens. After Doris came to get her tomorrow, then Milo would probably be back up in the bedroom, but for now, I was definitely flying solo.

The room felt even emptier after the moments Noah and I had shared here not too long ago, but we both had to work the next day, and I was also expecting Doris to be here at ten sharp. True, he

251

would have been long gone by then, since the clinic opened at 8 a.m., but still, it just seemed better to do it this way.

All the same, I had a feeling it wouldn't be too long before he was spending the night here...or I was staying over at his place.

But even though my private life seemed to be humming along just fine and it looked as if Cinny's woes about wanting a family had also been handled, I couldn't quite get Shelby Howard's voice out of my mind, how she'd said that Trevor had told her he'd figured out a way to guarantee them a bright future.

Clearly...tragically...it hadn't, but what had made him think everything was going to be just hunky-dory?

Since it didn't seem as if sleep was going to pay me a visit any time soon, I rolled over on my side and tried to recall every single thing I knew about the murder. There had been an attacker, probably male, who'd covered himself from head to toe in black, and who'd been able to keep his cool while stabbing his victim in the back with a sword.

Specifically, Trevor's sword, which had been taken from his office in the Miller & Miller building. It didn't sound as if he'd reported it stolen, which made me think it must have been absconded with shortly before he was murdered. Most likely, he hadn't even known the blade was missing.

All right. Technically, Miller & Miller had a standard eight-to-five schedule—I knew this because I'd seen their business hours posted on their website. True, there was always the chance that someone might have been working late that day, but maybe not on the floor where Trevor's office was located. If the murderer had waited until everyone had gone home for the day, would he have had enough time to drive to Salem and do the deed?

I stared at the bedroom ceiling and did some rough mental calculations. The crime was committed after Shelby and Trevor got back from dinner. It sounded as though they'd headed out a little after six, so, even though I didn't know what the medical examiner had put down as the time of death, I had to guess it was sometime between seven-thirty and eight. Since it only took about fifty minutes to drive from Boston to Salem—give or take—that meant the killer could have easily made it to the cottage and been lying in wait there within that span of time.

But how could the murderer have known Trevor was heading up to Salem? Obviously, I hadn't been there, but it felt to me as though the trip had been a spur-of-the-moment decision on Trevor's part. For whatever reason, he'd gotten to the psychological moment where it felt like it was the right time to sit down and have a talk with Shelby.

Exactly what had motivated him was still a complete unknown, as was the way the killer had managed to get the sword out of Trevor's office without anyone noticing. Even if he'd waited until the staff had gone home, there must have been a cleaning crew who was there. Also, how had the killer gotten past the building's security? Even during the day, I'd noticed a few security guards in the lobby, trying to look inconspicuous, but still definitely there. And I had to believe there was some kind of alarm system in place as well.

Maybe the killer's ex-CIA or something, I thought, my inner voice sounding grumpy even to me. Because, although I knew that utilizing former government agents was a favorite plot line in TV and movies, I kind of doubted Trevor Miller and the company he worked for were important enough to rate that kind of attention.

But who else would be able to get past the building's security in order to steal that sword?

Stare as I might at the ceiling, no answers appeared to be forthcoming. I released a huff of a breath, turned over again, and willed myself into sleep.

* * *

The next morning, I still felt cranky, especially since I hadn't had any prophetic dreams, hadn't experienced any flashes of insight. No, I wasn't psychic, but still, I'd kind of been hoping that maybe some burst of inspiration would have come swimming up out of my subconscious.

But because my subconscious seemed to have disappeared to the Seychelles for the time being, I went ahead and got out of bed, showered and washed my hair, and then headed downstairs. I knew I could be somewhat leisurely this morning, thanks to waiting around for Doris's ten o'clock arrival instead of hurrying out so I could be at the shop by no later than nine forty-five.

The animals were awake, although, since Cinny had all four kittens fastened to her and having their breakfast, she didn't stir from her bed. She still looked happy and content, and if the kittens had kept waking her up through the night so they could nurse, she didn't show any sign of it.

Milo, however, got up as soon as I walked into the kitchen. "Was everything quiet down here?" I asked, even though I knew the answer to that question.

"Mostly," he replied, and sent an amused glance in the kittens' direction. "Those little things can be pretty ear-piercing when they want a 2 a.m. feeding."

"I can imagine," I said dryly. "Thanks for doing guard duty."

"Well, I wanted Cinny to feel safe."

"And I did," she said, her gaze fixed on both of us. "We all did. Still," she added, pink nose twitching a bit, "I'd really like to get up and use the litter box."

"Well, let them finish feeding, and then Milo and I will keep an eye on them while you take care of business—and have some breakfast," I added, since I guessed she was probably hungry as well.

Cinny looked grateful for that offer, and since the kittens finished up not too long after that, she was able to attend to her own needs, and eat the bowl of canned Salmon Surprise I set out for her after that. Milo had his breakfast, too, and since I wasn't feeling too ambitious that morning, I settled for an English muffin with some homemade strawberry jam.

Afterward, I went upstairs to brush my teeth and put on my face, although, since this was a regular workday, that didn't take too long, just some mascara and a little bit of sheer lipstick. I was back downstairs by nine-thirty, which meant I still had plenty of time before Doris showed up.

The kittens were sleeping, so I didn't linger in the kitchen, only got myself a glass of water and headed back out to the living room. There wasn't much to do there, either, although I made sure the chairs were sitting straight at the dining room table and everything else was in order.

A quick peek past the curtains told me Doris wasn't here yet. She'd teleported to my house previously, something that very few witches could do, but I guessed she would be driving today. After all, it wouldn't be very easy to disappear herself out of here, not when she had to take Cinny and a litter of kittens back with her.

Because I still had about fifteen minutes to wait, I sat down on the sofa and got out the deck of Rider-Waite Tarot cards I kept in one of the coffee table's drawers. Unlike a lot of other witches, I generally didn't turn to the cards for advice, but I was restless now, feeling as though I needed to be doing something...even if I wasn't quite sure what that something should be.

Anyway, it was almost soothing to shuffle the cards and shuffle them again, even if I didn't really know what I was doing. Sure, I understood the meanings of the major arcana, but I'd never been very good at piecing together the information the minor cards were trying to convey.

All the same, I pulled out one card and laid it down on the table.

The King of Swords.

I felt myself frown. Under regular circumstances, I might not have thought there was anything especially noteworthy about that particular card. Now, though, with Trevor Miller's murder still fresh in my mind, I couldn't help thinking there was maybe a reason why I'd pulled out that card instead of one of the seventy-seven others in the deck.

Figuring I might as well play along, I pulled out another card and set it next to the card lying on the tabletop.

The Queen of Swords.

What the hell?

Okay, I supposed it wasn't statistically impossible to have pulled those cards in sequence. All the same, a little shiver ran down my spine.

What was going on here?

Third time's a charm, I thought, and pulled another card and set it down beside the other two.

The Knight of Swords.

Okay, this was getting ridiculous. Had I forgotten to shuffle the cards the last time I used them?

Even if I hadn't, that explanation didn't make any sense. The only way those three cards would have been next to each other in an unshuffled deck was if it was brand-new, and I knew that wasn't the case. I'd had these cards for years and years; my mother had given them to me on my sixteenth birthday, telling me that every witch needed to have a set of Tarot cards, even if that wasn't where her true powers lay. And although I didn't use them all that much, I still knew they must have been shuffled dozens and dozens of times between now and then.

I didn't have the chance to ponder the mystery any further, though, because the doorbell rang. Quickly, I picked up the cards and shoved them in the table's drawer, then rose from the sofa and went to open the door.

As expected, Doris Dalrymple was standing outside. She carried a big basket, one she obviously planned to use to transport Cinny and the kittens.

"Morning," I said, stepping aside so she could come in the house.

"Where's Cinny?" she asked.

Clearly, she didn't see the point in wasting time on pleasantries.

"In the kitchen, in her bed," I replied. "She seemed most comfortable there."

"And the kittens?"

"They're fine," I assured her. "I think they've gotten bigger already."

Doris gave me a head tilt in response to that comment, telling me she thought I might be exaggerating just a bit.

However, her stern expression faded as soon as she entered the kitchen and spied Cinny in her bed with the kittens snuggled up against her.

"Oh, they're adorable!"

That they were, especially the little calico girl

who'd already laid a special claim on my heart. But I knew I couldn't keep her, not when I already had Milo...and not when the next familiar who came through my door might not be as agreeable as he was about having a menagerie under my roof.

Cinny looked up at her mistress, green eyes glowing with pride. "I'm a good mother, aren't I?"

"The best," Doris replied at once. "Do you think you can help me get the kittens in the basket?"

"Absolutely."

The cat extricated herself from the pile of kittens, then carefully picked up each one by the scruff of its neck and gently placed it in the pile of blankets inside the basket. They mewed a bit at this treatment but seemed to understand they needed to cooperate, because none of them tried to escape.

Once they were all safely inside the basket, Cinny climbed in as well, and licked them a little to show she was still looking out for them and that they had nothing to worry about, even if they had been moved from their warm, comfortable spot in the kitchen.

I bent and picked up her bed and her bowls. "I can walk these out to the car for you."

"That would be wonderful," Doris replied. "Thank you."

After telling Milo he needed to stay in the house—he looked a little disappointed, but didn't protest—I followed Doris out to the Cadillac SUV parked at the curb. She opened the passenger door and deposited the basket on the seat, then secured it in place with the seat belt. After she was done, and after she'd given Cinny a gentle pat on the head, she turned back toward me.

"Thank you for what you did," she said, and I gave an embarrassed shrug.

"I'm sorry about springing the kittens on you —" I began, but Doris shook her head.

"It's fine," she cut in. "I haven't seen Cinny this happy in a long time. And it'll be fun to have the kittens underfoot. Who knows? I may even decide to keep them."

That comment made me stare at her in surprise, which I assumed was exactly what she'd intended. Smiling to herself, she headed around to the driver's side of the SUV, then climbed behind the wheel and started the engine.

I waved as Doris pulled away from the curb, even though I didn't know for sure whether either she or Cinny could see me. Still, I felt as though I needed to give them a proper goodbye.

When I went back inside the house, Milo was sitting next to the sofa, looking forlorn.

"I get it, buddy," I told him, and gave him a reassuring scratch behind his ears. "I'm going to miss them, too."

"We hardly got to have the kittens here at all," he complained.

"I know," I said. "But Cinny got what she'd been pining for...and you knew from the beginning that she wasn't going to live with us permanently."

Because Milo probably realized there wasn't much point in arguing with that comment, he just let out a little doggy sigh. "I suppose so." He stopped there and angled a glance up at me, big brown eyes curious. "Is it hard for you to say goodbye to the familiars you watch?"

"A little," I replied. "I mean, they're only with me for a week or so at the most, and because I go into it knowing that, it makes it a little easier. Mostly, I'm just glad that I've been able to help them and that they're going back to a life where things are going to work better for them and their mistresses. This one was probably hard for you because it was the first time you had to deal with all this."

"And Cinny was nice."

"Yes, she was," I agreed. "Mostly, familiars are."

Which was the truth. There had been one or two notable exceptions—including the Capuchin monkey who thought it was funny to tear the stuffing out of my sofa pillows and leave it all over the living room floor—but generally, familiars wanted to please humans, even the ones who weren't their mistresses.

"It still feels strange not to have to look out for Cinny," Milo said, and I leaned down to ruffle his ears again.

"Well, it's a nice day. You should go outside and lie in the sun. And maybe those squirrels who were hanging out in my yard a couple of weeks ago have decided to make a return appearance."

At my mention of the squirrels, Milo immediately perked up. Brown eyes shining, he said, "Yes, I need to check on that."

He bounded off toward the kitchen, and a moment later, I heard the dog door slam. Clearly, losing Cinny as a companion had upset him, but not so much that he couldn't still find amusement elsewhere.

Hoping he'd be occupied for at least a little while, I headed over to the sofa and sat down, then opened the coffee table drawer again. Inside were my Rider-Waite Tarot cards, scattered across the bottom of the drawer.

Had it been a fluke for me to get the King, Queen, and Knight of Swords all in a row? Or were the cards trying to tell me something?

Well, I knew what I had to do to find out.

I shuffled the cards several times before I decided they were probably mixed up enough for the original pull to be lost among the rest of the suits and major arcana. Holding my breath, I pulled a card.

The King of Swords.

Even I, who generally wasn't the sort of person always on the lookout for signs and portents, knew this couldn't be an accident. The odds against me pulling the same card again were just way too high.

Before I could lose my nerve, I pulled two more cards.

The Queen and Knight of Swords.

I sent a nervous glance over one shoulder, wondering if someone had decided to play a particularly annoying trick on me, but I knew I was alone in the house. There was no one else around to influence the cards, to compel me to choose the ones they wanted me to draw from the deck.

Should I stop there?

No, something was telling me I needed to go on.

I pulled three more cards.

The Tower, the Devil, and the Five of Swords, the one that showed a man lying prone on a lonely road, five swords sticking out of his back.

Just like what had happened to Trevor Miller... although his killer had settled for using just the one blade.

And it wasn't as though the Tower and the Devil were exactly friendly cards, either. The Tower usually meant some kind of dramatic, often terrible, kind of change was coming, or had already happened. The appearance of the Devil in a reading was usually an indication of some kind of temptation, but it could also mean a feeling of powerlessness, of being trapped.

Was that how Trevor had been feeling at work? What had changed to make him tell Shelby he thought they had a great future to look forward to?

And why the King, Queen, and Knight of Swords?

As I stared down at them, a sick feeling stirred in the pit of my stomach. I didn't want to think such a thing, didn't want to entertain such a horrible notion for even a second, but....

I picked up the King of Swords and gazed at it for a long moment. The image showed a stern-faced man sitting on a throne, an upraised sword held in his right hand. The set of the king's jaw seemed to tell me he had little mercy to spare for anyone who didn't obey his rules.

In that moment, I knew, with a terrible sinking certainty in the pit of my stomach.

Thad Miller had murdered his son.

Chapter 16

Sins of the Father

The King of Swords card fell from my numb fingers and fluttered to the floor, but I didn't bend down to pick it up. Now that I'd acknowledged the horrible truth, it all made an awful kind of sense.

Trevor must have gone to his father and told him he wanted to come clean about how the associates at the firm had been covering up for him. Maybe Thad had been angry, or maybe he'd acted as though he was on board with his son's plan. Since I hadn't been there—and I kind of doubted I'd be allowed to conduct a scrying session in the offices of Miller & Miller to find out for sure—this was all pure conjecture on my part, but it made sense. Either way, it seemed as though Trevor had thought he'd cleared the air with his father, and that was why he'd come to Salem to tell Shelby everything was going to be just fine.

Only, it definitely was anything but fine. Thad must have been convinced that such an announcement would be the ruin of a company that had been his family's business for generations, and had decided it was better to lose his son than lose everything his ancestors had worked so hard for.

And of course it would be easy enough for him to take the sword from Trevor's office. Thad probably had a master key that allowed him access to pretty much anything in the building, and if he waited until everyone else was gone, it wasn't as though he'd have to explain to his employees why he was removing the blade from his son's private office.

I didn't know how Thad had sneaked the sword out of the building—an overcoat? not exactly inconspicuous in June, but better than walking through the lobby with a naked blade— but in the end, I supposed it didn't matter so much.

No, what mattered was that he'd driven north to Salem, murder in his heart, and had waited for Trevor and Shelby to come back from dinner so he could get rid of his troublesome son once and for all.

Problem was, even though this all made plenty of sense to me, I had absolutely no idea how I could possibly prove any of it. If Thad Miller was a cool enough customer to lie in wait and then drive a sword through his son's back, I kind of doubted he would break down and confess all to me.

Okay, there had to be some other way around all this.

I thought of Lorna Miller then, how she'd told me she and her husband no longer had need of my services. Had they gotten rid of me out of pure frustration, or had they only enlisted my services to muddy the water and make sure Thad got away with the crime?

The thought had its own terrible logic. After all, why could anyone believe that a guilty party would want to hire a detective to solve the crime he himself had committed?

And if Lorna was her husband's accomplice, then she was also the world's greatest actress.

Because I didn't know what else to do, I picked up the card I'd dropped and the others from the card pull that still lay on the coffee table, then shuffled them back into the deck and returned it to its usual spot in the table's drawer. There didn't seem to be much point in preserving the layout; it wasn't as though I could take a photo of it, show it to the police, and say, "See? This is how I proved Thad Miller killed his son."

All right, then...how *could* I prove this? Mr. Miller had been careful not to leave any physical evidence at the scene of the crime, or the police would have found it. No, it seemed like the only thing that could possibly work was a confession, and I already knew that wasn't going to happen.

My thoughts returned to Lorna Miller. Maybe she was the weak link in all this. If she was privy to her husband's crime but was covering it up because he'd coerced her or simply because she was weak and didn't want to lose the comfortable lifestyle he'd given her, then maybe it would be a lot easier to back her into a corner, make her tell me the terrible secret she'd been hiding.

And I knew exactly how I needed to do it.

* * *

Truth potions weren't really that difficult to make. Their one drawback was that the person who'd drunk the potion would remember everything they'd said while under its influence, but no enchantment was perfect. We witches tended to avoid using them, just as we generally tried to avoid casting spells that involved dubious consent, like love enchantments of any sort, because doing so was entering a very morally gray area.

In this particular case, though, I thought I'd get a pass.

Of course, getting Lorna to blurt out all her secrets to me wouldn't do any good if I didn't have

a recording of her doing so, and because Massachusetts didn't allow conversations to be
recorded unless both parties had agreed to it, I
knew I'd have to record her saying she was all right
with having her words captured if I had any
chance of handing her confession over to the
police.

Well, unless I wanted to get arrested myself.

But the nice thing about truth potions was that
they tended to make the person who'd drunk them
highly suggestible, so as long as I could get Lorna to
drink the stuff in the first place, I could simply ask
her for permission before we got down to the real
meat of our conversation.

No, the hard part would be getting her to agree
to see me at all.

I'd told Sage I'd be in late, but now I needed to
let her know I wasn't sure when I'd make it to
work, since I had to get this thing with Lorna
Miller handled before I did anything else.

"Let me guess," Sage said as soon as she picked
up. "You're going to be in later than you thought."

"Bingo," I replied.

"Is everything okay with Cinny?"

"Oh, she's fine," I replied. "Doris picked her up
a little while ago. I just have something else I need
to take care of today. Are things really crazy there?"

"No, it's pretty mellow for a Friday," Sage
assured me. "I think a lot of people did their trav-

eling over Memorial Day weekend. So I should be okay."

Not for the first time, I reflected how lucky I was that I'd hired Sage as my shop assistant. She'd come with great recommendations, and as a fellow member of the Salem witch community, she could be trusted to keep any sensitive conversations to herself, but I still hadn't known how great she'd be at covering for me at the shop when non-work matters claimed my time.

"I'll definitely be in tomorrow, though," I said, and I thought I heard a very small chuckle on the other end of the line, as if to say she'd believe it when she saw it.

All she told me, though, was "okay," and we ended the call there.

With that part of the logistics handled, I knew I needed to reach out to Lorna Miller. There was a very good chance she'd shoot me down, but I hoped if I phrased things correctly, she'd be concerned enough about what I might know that she'd agree to see me in person.

Because even though truth potions were generally very effective, they definitely didn't work long distance.

I navigated to my contacts list and located Lorna's number. There was always the possibility that she wouldn't pick up, that she'd let my call roll to voicemail once she realized who it was, but I had to hope for the best.

Her phone rang three times, and I bit my lip, rapidly composing a message that would be just as effective as actually talking to her.

But then I heard her crisp, cool tones coming through my phone's tiny speaker. "Charity Hughes. This is a surprise."

I supposed it was, considering she'd probably thought I was out of her life for good. "Hi, Lorna. I'm sorry to bother you, but we need to talk."

"We do?" she said, voice still unruffled. "I'm not sure about what. And I'm very busy—Trevor's funeral is Sunday."

The day after tomorrow. I supposed she probably did have about a million things to handle today, because the death of such a prominent member of the community—especially one who'd died so young—wasn't the kind of thing where a small, family-only kind of service would be acceptable.

I swallowed, and told myself I still didn't know whether Lorna was complicit in Trevor's death or not. That meant I had to put on my big-girl panties and do what needed to be done.

"I'm sorry," I said briefly. "But I just found something that we should probably talk about…in person."

She didn't reply right away, and I held my

breath, wondering what I would do if she called my bluff.

But then she said, "It's that important?"

"It is."

An edge of annoyance entered her tone. "And you expect me to drive all the way to Salem while I'm in the middle of planning Trevor's service?"

"No, no," I said hastily. "I can come to your house."

Another of those hesitations, and then she said, "All right. Can you be here in an hour?"

That was cutting it pretty close, but still doable. I didn't allow myself an exhalation of relief, however, and only said, "Sure. I'll need your address, though."

She rattled off an address in Beacon Hill, which didn't surprise me too much. Yes, there were other neighborhoods in the city that might have been more expensive, but it was still one of the richest and most established...and not too far from Shelby's house. I had to hope the two women wouldn't bump into each other while taking a walk or something, because that might be awkward.

"I'm leaving right now," I said.

"Then I'll see you in a bit."

We ended the call there, and, phone in hand, I hurried into the kitchen to grab my purse and stick my head out the back door. Milo was lying in the sun near a flowerbed, and I called out to him, "Hey,

Milo! I have to run to Boston. Will you be all right here by yourself?"

He raised his head. "Of course. But you'll be home for supper, right?"

"Absolutely," I replied. After all, I didn't see how this errand to Lorna Miller's house could possibly take that long. "And I'll put some food in your bowl right now for lunch."

His tail wagged, and I went ahead and closed the door, knowing that Milo could come and go through his doggy door. As I filled his bowl, I reflected that I was going to be running to Boston right in the middle of lunch...and I somehow doubted Lorna was going to offer to feed me.

But because I knew I didn't have time to even grab some fast food on the way down, I settled for tossing a granola bar in my purse right before I headed out. I'd already secured the vial of truth potion in an inner pocket of my bag, so I was as prepared as I could be.

If only my stomach wasn't so clenched with nervousness.

Luckily, traffic was kind of light for a Friday, so I made good time and didn't have to deal with any drama on the road. Winding my way toward Lorna's house took a little extra time, especially since I had to park a couple of blocks away. Despite those small delays, I was still standing on her front doorstep at almost exactly noon...

although I doubted she'd appreciate my timeliness.

The house was a big brick edifice on a corner, its style more late Victorian than the federal and neoclassical architecture that dominated so much of the older parts of Boston. That made sense, though, considering the elder Miller had made his name—and, I presumed, his fortune—building houses in the nineteenth century.

I'd halfway expected a housekeeper or some other hired help to open the door, but no, Lorna herself answered my knock. Just like the first time I'd met her, she looked impeccable, from her black sleeveless dress to the slender sling-back sandals on her feet, although today she wore black Tahitian pearls on her ears rather than the oversized diamond studs she'd had on during our first meeting.

"Come in," she said coolly.

Almost immediately to the left was a front parlor overlooking the street, with a marble fireplace surrounded by a carved walnut mantel dominating one side. The walls were painted a cheerful yellow, but they didn't do much to improve my mood as Lorna indicated that I should sit on one of the ivory-upholstered couches.

But even though I could tell she wasn't overly thrilled to have me there, that didn't mean she was going to ignore her role as hostess. "Some iced tea or lemonade?"

"Iced tea," I said immediately, and hoped she would be drinking the same thing. I didn't think lemonade would be quite acidic enough to mess with my potion, but it might still be a problem.

Lorna nodded and headed out of the room. A quick glance around told me the landscapes on the wall were probably originals, as was the furniture. Not heavy, ornate Victorian pieces, but what looked like more delicate and livable selections from probably half a century earlier. Had someone bought those later on, or had the original Miller who'd built this house decided he wanted the decor to harken back to an earlier era?

If I'd come here for purely social reasons, maybe I would have asked. As it was, I only sat there, vial of potion already removed from its inner pocket and slid under part of my skirt where it spread across the sofa cushion.

Good thing I'd done that so quickly, because Lorna returned a moment later, a glass of iced tea in each hand. She set the glasses down on some coasters that had already been waiting on the marble-topped table, then took a seat opposite me, her expression expectant.

"So," she said, "what was so important that you had to drive all the way down here to speak to me?"

"It's about Trevor," I replied.

Her gaze didn't flicker, but I didn't know whether that was because she truly didn't have a guilty conscience, or because she had such iron control over herself that she wouldn't allow even a single betraying movement.

"What about Trevor?"

Now was the time.

Not here but over there
Not in front, but anywhere
Look aside
Don't try to hide

As soon as I murmured the "look over there" spell, Lorna glanced over her shoulder, as though distracted by a vehicle passing on the street outside. I pulled out the vial and poured half its contents into her iced tea, then quickly stuck it back in my purse just as she turned back toward me.

"I think I've learned something interesting," I said, and picked up my iced tea and took a sip.

As I'd hoped, she reached for her own glass and sipped from it as well. At once, something in her eyes changed, the pupils enlarged, her gaze somehow blurred.

Perfect.

I reached into my purse and got out my phone, set it on the coffee table with fingers that only trembled a little bit, and activated the voice-memo app.

"Lorna Miller, do you mind if I record our conversation?" I asked.

"No, that's fine," she said. Like her expression, her voice was almost dreamy, very unlike her usual brisk self.

Well, hopefully the cops wouldn't notice that part.

Since it looked like the potion was doing its job, I didn't see the point in beating around the bush. "Lorna, did your husband Thad kill your son Trevor?"

A single blink. Then she said, "Yes."

Oh, my God. It was one thing to imagine such a horrible scenario, and something entirely different to hear the ugly truth of the matter stated so baldly. My stomach clenched, and I was suddenly glad I hadn't eaten that granola bar on my drive down here.

"Why?" I asked, even as I told myself that I needed to keep it together.

Lorna sipped some more of her iced tea. Yes, the potion had already done its job, but I knew that adding some more of the mixture to her bloodstream couldn't hurt. "Because he was going to tell the truth."

"About how he sucked as an architect and had his associates covering for him?"

A very small tremor went through her, and she released a melancholy sigh. "Yes, that. Thad said it would destroy the firm, would ruin us financially."

"So...you knew what he had planned?"

At once, Lorna gave a vehement shake of her head. "No. If I'd known, I would have tried to stop him. All he said was that he was going to Salem to try to talk some sense into our son. I told him that he should wait, that Trevor had gone up there to reconcile with Shelby, but Thad was furious. He said he couldn't wait, because he didn't know when Trevor might start saying the wrong things to the wrong people."

She paused there, and set her glass back down on its coaster, putting it in the exact center as though its placement was the most important thing in the world. Maybe it was. Better to focus on something insignificant than have to acknowledge that your husband had killed his own son.

"And after Trevor was found dead...?" I let the word trail off, mostly because I didn't know exactly what I should say. Surely Lorna must have suspected her husband, even if he hadn't confessed to her.

Her face twisted, showing what it probably would have looked like without the expert applications of Botox and fillers. "I didn't want to believe Thad could do such a thing," she said, her voice dropping to almost a whisper. I could only hope the voice recorder on my iPhone would continue to pick it up, although I tried to reassure myself that she'd already uttered the words that would lead to her husband's conviction, and anything she added now was basically icing on the cake.

"Did you ask him?" I knew my voice sounded hard, but I didn't care. It was much more unnerving than I'd imagined it would be to sit there and listen to her confession, and now I just wanted to gather as much information as I could so I could get the hell out of here and back to Salem, away from this nightmare.

"No," she said. She crossed her arms and held them tightly against her stomach, although I didn't know whether she made the gesture to protect herself or because she was cold, chilled to the bone at the thought of what her husband had done. "I didn't have to. I saw it in his eyes when the police called us to tell us Trevor was dead. There wasn't a hint of surprise. Thad had been expecting that call."

"But you didn't confront him over it."

She shook her head. "How could I? If I could have stopped him, I would have, but once it was done...." The words faded away, as if she'd somehow realized that to say anything else would only incriminate her as well. "I had our daughter to think of. If everyone thought this was a terrible tragedy and nothing else, then eventually, we'd be able to go on with our lives."

How she would have been able to lie down next to her husband every night knowing he was the one who'd killed their son, I had no idea. Yes, people truly were masters of self-deception, but that was going awfully far.

Not that it mattered. I had the evidence I needed, and now I just wanted to get far, far away from this pretty room with its ugly secrets, back to my cheerful house and the dog who waited for me there.

And to Noah. Maybe if I were back in his arms, I'd be able to forget all of this.

I reached for my phone and shut off the voice memo, then stood up as I shoved the iPhone in my purse. "You've been very helpful, Lorna," I said, making my voice as soothing as possible. While a truth potion wouldn't allow a person to do something that was truly against their nature, they were still highly suggestible while under its influence.

And I needed to use that to my advantage now.

"I need to get going," I said. "You can sit here and wait."

"Wait for what?" she asked, although the resignation in her tone told me she knew exactly who she'd be waiting for.

"Just wait," I repeated, and headed for the front door.

She didn't try to stop me.

* * *

The drive back to Salem felt interminable, but maybe that was because the Friday afternoon traffic had already started to stack up, even though I'd spent less than a half hour at Lorna's Beacon Hill house.

Thad Miller really had murdered his son, and his wife had known and done nothing to turn him in. Not out of some kind of twisted, misplaced loyalty, but because she didn't want anything to disturb her comfortable life.

I didn't go home when I got to town, though. No, I headed straight for the main police headquarters on Margin Street.

A deputy who looked like she was probably around my age but much more businesslike sat at the front desk. "Can I help you?" she asked politely.

"I need to talk to whoever is handling the Trevor Miller murder case," I said. "I have some new evidence for them."

"Detective Falco?" the deputy said, looking startled. She had big brown eyes and black braided hair pulled back into a thick ponytail.

Right. I recognized the name as the same one mentioned in several pieces about the murder in our local paper, although I didn't know anything else about the man.

"Yes, that's him," I said.

"Just a moment."

She picked up the phone that sat on her desk, dialed an extension, and waited for a few seconds. The detective in question must have answered, because the deputy then said, "Detective Falco? I have someone here who says she has information about the Miller case." A pause, and she said, "Sure. I'll let her know."

The deputy replaced the handset in the receiver, and I gave her an inquiring look.

"He'll be right out," she told me.

Sure enough, a man in a white button-up shirt, khakis, and a slightly askew tie entered the lobby just a minute later. The detective's name had made me think he must be some grizzled veteran right out of a classic cop show, but that presumption couldn't have been more off the mark. This Detective Falco looked like he was probably just a couple of years older than I was, with thick dark hair and dark eyes, and wouldn't have been out of place modeling for Armani or something.

Or maybe playing on the Italian soccer team.

"Hi, there," he said, and extended a hand. "Detective Falco."

"Charity Hughes," I replied, glad I hadn't been

put so off balance by his appearance that I couldn't muster a normal response.

"Deputy Thomas said you have something on the Miller case?"

"I do," I said. "But we should probably talk about it in private."

He didn't miss a beat. "Sure," he said. "We can go to my office. This way."

And he led me out of the lobby and down a short corridor, then another. Almost immediately after making the turn, he opened a door for me.

"Right in here."

His office seemed pretty typical—computer and printer, stacks of file folders sitting on the desk. However, the walls were covered with posters of travel scenes, and not the wanted posters or public-service announcement kind of stuff I'd been expecting.

"Have a seat."

I took the chair he'd indicated...the only one in the office besides the one behind the desk, which was where he seated himself.

"So," he said, after we were both situated, "what's this all about?"

In answer, I reached into my purse and got out my iPhone. "I have a recording where Lorna Miller implicates her husband in the murder of their son."

One of Detective Falco's black brows lifted just

the slightest bit. "Did you have her permission to make the recording?"

"I did," I said imperturbably. "Listen for yourself."

Leaning forward, I set the phone on his desk, opened the voice memo app, and touched the screen to start the playback. As he listened, the detective's brows drew together, but he didn't say anything, only sat there expressionless until we reached the end of the recording.

For a moment longer, he remained silent. Then he said, "Why would Lorna Miller confess all this to you?"

"Guilty conscience?" I suggested, and the faintest hint of a smile touched Detective Falco's sculpted mouth.

"Possibly." A pause, and he added, "And why did you even get the idea to talk to her?"

"Because she and her husband asked me to investigate Trevor's murder," I said frankly. "Now I'm pretty sure they were just hoping my involvement would muddy the waters, would make it harder for the authorities to figure out what actually happened to their son."

The smile disappeared, but otherwise, the detective didn't seem to have any real reaction to my words. Was it possible he knew something about the way I'd managed to track down Darla Fitzgerald's murderer? There wasn't any reason for the Salem police department to have been involved with that investigation, since it involved a crime that had taken place a thousand miles from their jurisdiction, but....

To my relief, he didn't seem inclined to ask any other questions along that line, because he went on, "I assume you don't want me to confiscate your phone, so I'm asking your permission to make a copy of the recording. I'll also need you to sign an affidavit attesting that the recording hasn't been edited or altered in any way."

Yikes. I hadn't even imagined that the police might try to seize my phone, or that they would need me to state that the recording hadn't been tampered with. Then again, I wasn't exactly in the business of taping people's confessions.

"Sure, make as many copies as you like," I told him.

"This'll take a few minutes," he said. "Just hang tight."

The detective picked up my phone and headed out of the office, presumably to a lab or something where they had the kind of equipment you'd need to make a copy of a voice recording. It felt weird to sit there, waiting and doing nothing, but since Detective Falco had my phone, it wasn't like I could check my emails or Instagram or whatever.

I wasn't wearing a watch, but he had a clock on one wall in between a gorgeous poster of the Isle of

Capri and a place I couldn't identify, probably somewhere in the Alps, all snowy and pristine. That was how I knew it took almost ten minutes for him to finish duplicating the recording before he returned to the office and handed my phone back to me.

"All done," he said as I took the phone and put it back in my purse.

"So...what happens now?" I asked.

He smiled, but something about that smile told me he was still deadly serious.

"Now I get to pay a little visit to the Millers."

Chapter 17

It's Complicated

ut Detective Falco never got to have that talk with Thad and Lorna Miller. Yes, he drove down to Boston and went to their house, only to find a sobbing, barely coherent Lorna there. Someone from the firm had just called her and told her there had been a single gunshot in Thad's office at the Miller & Miller offices downtown. When his assistant rushed in to see what had happened, it was to find her boss slumped over his desk, a single bullet hole in his temple.

He'd left a note, of course, a note that claimed all responsibility for Trevor's death and made sure to clarify that Lorna had nothing to do with the terrible crime. That note had carefully sidestepped mentioning any reason for killing his son, stating only that they had "differences."

I could read between the lines, though. Thad

had wanted to use that sword to murder Trevor because he viewed his son's intention to tell the truth about his abilities as the very worst sort of backstabbing. A personal killing needed a personal weapon, hence the reason why Thad had used Trevor's sword to carry out his revenge, even though an anonymous one bought on the internet would have been worlds safer.

Based on what was in the note and the conversation I'd recorded with Lorna, the Salem P.D. decided not to pursue charges against her, even though it sounded as though there might have been some basis for claiming she'd been an accessory after the fact.

Maybe even the police had decided she'd lost enough already.

I saw all this in the local paper, obviously, because although Detective Falco had seemed friendly enough when I brought him the recording, he didn't have any real reason to drop by and discuss the case with me. And Shelby, although shaken, according to Noah, had recovered enough to attend Trevor's funeral on Sunday.

"They'll have to have another one for Thad," Noah told me when I came over to help him get set up for our barbecue with Jared and Kathy. We'd discussed canceling it, considering everything that had happened over the past few days, but because we hadn't known either of the victims, we'd decided there wasn't much point in pretending that we were grieving their loss. "Something quiet, I suppose."

Very quiet. Reports were that the firm had been left to Lorna in Thad's will, but I had no idea what she planned to do with it. If I were her, I'd find a responsible buyer for the business, someone who could carry on its legacy but be separate from the scandal and tragedy that had marked its final days.

But that was her decision to make, I supposed.

"It's a horrible mess," I said. "But I'm glad Shelby is doing better."

"She's relieved that she's been completely exonerated," Noah told me. "But she also doesn't know what to do next, which I get. She thought she was going to have a future with Trevor, but now...."

The words trailed off, and he shook his head before picking up the bowl of Boston baked beans I'd brought over so he could take it out to the table on the deck. Jared and Kathy were due to be here at any moment, and the bowl of beans was one of the last things that needed to be put in place. A few moments earlier, when I'd gone outside to lay down the placemats and arrange the melamine plates and drinkware, I'd murmured a quiet spell under my breath to keep the flies and mosquitoes away, so at least we wouldn't have to worry about any biting insects during our meal.

"I'm sure Shelby will figure it out," I said. "She seems like a pretty strong woman."

"She is," Noah agreed. "And it's not as if she doesn't have her own resources. But it's still a tough situation to be in."

I made a sound of agreement, and we had to leave the conversation there, since the doorbell rang and we needed to put on our company faces.

And that was fine. I was all too ready to put tragedy behind me and have a normal get-together with friends. Even a few weeks ago, I would never have thought this would be my life now—a barbecue at Noah's place, sitting down with people whose company I enjoyed and not having to worry about anything other than the here and now.

I didn't know how long this was all going to last, but I figured I'd enjoy it while I could.

More details emerged about Trevor's murder, as they usually did. It appeared that Thad Miller had smuggled his son's sword out of his office in the kind of large portfolio they used at the firm to carry blueprints, so of course no one had noticed anything strange about that. No, he'd just slid the sword in there, said goodnight to the security guards in the lobby as he left the building, and headed to Salem to carry out his murderous plans.

He'd been careful; it wasn't as though he'd gone online to buy the black getup he'd used to disguise himself, or the lock-pick set that had been found in his desk drawer at home. But those ninja masks were easy enough to purchase at martial-arts supply stores, and if he'd paid cash, obviously there wouldn't have been any record of the transaction.

As it had turned out, he hadn't needed the lock picks, since Shelby had unwittingly left the cottage door unlocked. But even if she'd been more careful, Thad would still have been able to get inside one way or another.

And the gun he'd used to end his life and make sure he'd never spend a single day in jail was one he'd bought legally years before, claiming he wanted it for home defense purposes. Maybe when he first purchased it, that had been his only intention, even if it had turned out to also be a means of escape for him.

As to why he used Trevor's sword to kill his son, when some other weapon would have probably have served his purpose much better, no one really seemed to know, since that twisted secret had gone with Thad to his grave. I still believed that Thad thought Trevor was stabbing him in the back, and therefore he wanted to literally do that very thing to his child. Wielding a blade that had been one of his son's prized possessions was probably just the black cherry on a very dark sundae.

But after those few follow-up articles in the local paper, everyone in town appeared to move on from the incident. That made sense, I supposed; Trevor Miller's death hadn't affected any of Salem's residents directly, except maybe poor Hannah Owens, who now had to disclose on her vacation rental's listings on Airbnb and VRBO that someone had been murdered there. She'd actually muttered a few times that she was thinking of selling the place, since she'd had a couple of cancellations, and she feared the little house would no longer be worth maintaining.

"Well, wait and see how Halloween goes," I told her when she dropped into Full Moon Apothecary for a refill on her arthritis tincture. "People would probably love to stay in a haunted cottage then."

"It is *not* haunted," Hannah retorted. "I've walked through the entire place and haven't felt anything strange at all."

It was on the tip of my tongue to tell Hannah she wasn't really a medium, and therefore it was possible she couldn't really be a hundred-percent certain on that point. I refrained, though, mostly because I knew I hadn't sensed anything when I was at the cottage, either. And while I also couldn't claim to be a medium or even all that psychic, I figured if two witches had been in the place and neither one of them had felt anything off about the cottage, then it was probably just fine.

"Yes," I said with a grin, "but if you put in the listing that it's haunted, I'll bet you'll get people lining up to rent the place."

That suggestion seemed to cheer her right up, because she nodded and said that sounded like a wonderful idea. As she hurried out, paper bag with her tincture held in one hand, probably the last person I would have expected to visit my shop brushed past her.

Detective Falco.

I blinked at him, then managed, "Can I help you find something?"

He smiled. No, his smiles didn't have the same brilliance as Noah's, but there was still something kind of velvety and fascinating about them nonetheless.

"Oh, I was in the area and thought I'd drop by. I realized I never really thanked you for providing that recording of Lorna Miller's confession."

About all I could do was shrug. "Well, I don't know if her confession really helped all that much. I mean, it was the note Thad Miller left behind that really clinched things, wasn't it?"

Detective Falco removed his sunglasses and slid them into his breast pocket. His eyes were as night-dark as his hair, such a contrast to Noah's piercing sky blue. "I don't know about that. I'm pretty sure if we didn't have her confession as leverage, he might not have felt the need to tell the real truth about what happened."

Maybe so. Not for the first time, the uncomfortable thought slid through my mind that if I hadn't gone and talked to Lorna, hadn't given her the potion so she'd tell the truth about the situation, Thad Miller might not have felt compelled to take his own life.

You can't feel guilty about that, I told myself. *It's not like you made him stab his son in the back, or made him cover up what an awful architect Trevor was.*

True enough. I still didn't like it, though.

"Anyway," the detective went on, "that's not the whole reason why I came by today."

"It isn't?" I responded. He didn't seem like the type who would use folk remedies for his various aches and pains, but if I'd learned anything in this life, it was that people would continue to surprise me, probably until I was dead.

"No," he said, and smiled again. "I realized we were never properly introduced. Derek Falco."

And he reached out a hand. I took it and gave it a little shake, since I wasn't sure what else to do. His fingers were strong, but he wasn't one of those guys who felt the need to crush your hand when exchanging a shake.

"Now that we have that out of the way," he went on, "I wanted to ask you something."

"Um...sure," I said. This whole exchange felt a little weird, and I found myself glad that Hannah had left and I'd sent Sage out to get us some sandwiches for lunch, since it was nearly one o'clock. At least this way, I didn't have anyone around watching this somehow awkward conversation.

Derek Falco's dark eyes glinted, and his mouth curved in a small smile. "I was wondering if maybe you'd like to have dinner with me."

I stared at him for a second, and then the import of his words sank in.

Oh, boy, I thought.

* * *

Charity's adventures will continue in *Hexes and Hedgehogs,* releasing in November 2023.

Social Medium

Household Demons

Perpetual Potion

Jingle Spells

Wandering Monsters

Uninvited Ghosts

Prophet Motive

Ballroom Bits

Spell Check

Charm School (February 2024)

UNEXPECTED MAGIC*

(Urban Fantasy/Paranormal Romance)

Found Objects

Finders, Keepers

Lost and Found

Finding Destiny

THE WITCHES OF WHEELER PARK*

(Paranormal Romance)

Storm Born

Thunder Road

Winds of Change

Mind Games

A Wheeler Park Christmas

Blood Ties

Healing Hands

Wishful Thinking

Smoke and Mirrors

* * *

MISS PRIMM'S ACADEMY FOR WAYWARD
WITCHES*

(Fantasy/Academy Romance)

Misspelled

Dispelled

Expelled

* * *

PROJECT DEMON HUNTERS*

(Paranormal Romance)

Unquiet Souls

Unbound Spirits

Unholy Ground

Unseen Voices

Unmarked Graves

Unbroken Vows

* * *

THE DEVIL YOU KNOW*

(Paranormal Romance)

Sympathy for the Devil

Charmed, I'm Sure

A Wing and a Prayer

Wish Upon a Star

* * *

THE WITCHES OF CANYON ROAD*

(Paranormal Romance)

Hidden Gifts

Darker Paths

Mysterious Ways

A Canyon Road Christmas

Demon Born

An Ill Wind

Higher Ground

Haunted Hearts

* * *

Fallen

Broken

Forsaken

Forbidden

Awoken

Illuminated

Stolen

Forgotten

Driven

Unspoken

THE WATCHERS TRILOGY*

(Paranormal Romance)

Falling Dark

Dead of Night

Rising Dawn

THE SEDONA FILES*

(Paranormal/Science Fiction Romance)

Bad Vibrations

Desert Hearts

Angel Fire

Star Crossed

Falling Angels

Enemy Mine

* * *

TALES OF THE LATTER KINGDOMS*

(Fantasy Romance)

All Fall Down

Dragon Rose

Binding Spell

Ashes of Roses

One Thousand Nights

Threads of Gold

The Wolf of Harrow Hall

Moon Dance

The Song of the Thrush

* * *

THE GAIAN CONSORTIUM SERIES*

(Science Fiction Romance)

Beast (free prequel novella)

Blood Will Tell

Breath of Life

The Gaia Gambit

The Mandala Maneuver

The Titan Trap

The Zhore Deception

The Refugee Ruse

* * *

STANDALONE TITLES

Hearts on Fire (Paranormal Romance)

Taking Dictation (Contemporary Romance)

Golden Heart (Gaslight Fantasy Romance)

Night Music: A Modern Reimagining of The Phantom of the Opera (Contemporary Romance)

Ghost Dance: A Sequel to Gaston Leroux's The Phantom of the Opera (Historical Mystery/Romance)

Flight Before Christmas (Fantasy Romance)

* Indicates a completed series

About the Author

USA Today bestselling author Christine Pope has been writing stories ever since she commandeered her family's Smith-Corona typewriter back in grade school. Her work includes paranormal romance, cozy paranormal mystery, and urban fantasy, among others. She makes her home in New Mexico.

Christine Pope on the Web:
www.christinepope.com

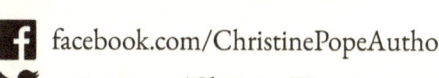 facebook.com/ChristinePopeAuthor
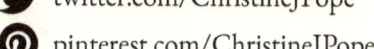 twitter.com/ChristineJPope
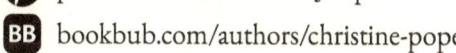 pinterest.com/ChristineJPope
bookbub.com/authors/christine-pope

www.ingramcontent.com/pod-product-compliance
Lightning Source LLC
Chambersburg PA
CBHW020410260626
47156CB00007B/2317